MURDERED BY MISTAKE

Freestone Series

Book 4

This is a fictitious Virginia novel which includes mystery, suspense, murder, romance, and a lot of humor, pets, and a sprinkle of the paranormal.

Faye M. Benjamin

DEDICATION

This book is dedicated to William & Sandra Johnson, Jr.,
Alfred & Barbara Johnson,
Larry & Lucille Sears,
Ike & Carolyn Meiggs

In memory of Clara Sears Leary, Ann Sears Meads,
Edna Meads, Lucy Sears Lee, Halsey Sears,
Pearl Sears Meiggs, Dillworth Sears, and Milton Sears

Freestone List of Characters

Director of Freestone: Dolly Hamilton

Deputy Director of Freestone: Dan Kramer

Dolly's secretary and cousin: Desiree Waverly

Supervisor of the IT Department: Shontelle Davis
IT Department: Diana Ripley

Supervisor of Cyber Security: Jason Hartman
Cyber Security: Alicia Decatur

Supervisor of Forensic Lab: Dr. Heather Burfoot

Supervisor of Photo Lab: Julie Tsai

Supervisors of Safe House Network:
Millie Kramer, Mabel Langley, and Mandy Logan

Supervisor of Investigative Teams: Vince Chappell

Supervisor of Surveillance/ Security Teams: Chad Napier

Supervisor of Covert Missions: Ted Osborne

Training Officer: Shiloh Casey

Receptionist: Sierra Chase

Financial Officer: Art Hamilton

Investigative Team 7: Ryan Creekmore and Brad Donahue

Freestone Security Agents: Byron Sawyer, Adam Cobb, and
Cody McCaslin

LIST OF CHARACTERS

Timothy Bronner/Greta Bronner

Dr. Kurt Bronner/ Emily Bronner

Dr. Duane Newby/Karen Newby

Dr. Michael Lim

Dr. Maxine Stine

Dr. Elwood Harris/Dr. Clara Beach/Dr. Rose Smith/

Dr. Roy Tanner

Maria Santana

Vernell Cleveland

Dillon Carr

Hansa Fareed

Emma Baker

Harry Dent/Jesse Rice

Dr. Colin Zocrist

Becky Anderson

David Gatewood

Sheridan Chase/Sierra Chase

Erika Conrad

Gil Sawyer

Detective Gage/Detective Hansen

Chief Ramsey/Sheriff Patterson

Nurse Isa, Nurse Lucy, Nurse Lottie

Ernesto & Rosarita Gomez

Ruth Parrish

Judge Franklin/Deanna Perry

Nathan Donovan/Vickie Donovan Tierney

Sheriff Patterson/Chief Ramsey

Pixie & Dixie

John & Wendy Madison/Heidi Madison/Hunter Madison

Jim & Penny Vogel/Aidan Vogel

John Meadows/Taylor W. Meadows

Summary

The deputy CEO of Bronner Pharmaceuticals is killed in a car accident during a fierce storm. Was it an accident or murder? Three months later, the owner and CEO of Bronner Pharmaceuticals, Dr. Kurt Bronner, his pregnant wife, and daughter are murdered in their home execution style.

Five year old Timothy Bronner is led through the woods behind his house by a special friend to get help for his family, even though he doesn't know what has happened to them. After walking a mile and a half through thick trees and underbrush, he is led to Millie Kramer's farmhouse. Household members rush to the little boy as he collapses from exhaustion before he can reach the house.

Freestone Investigations and Security, and police from two counties rush to protect little Timmy and catch the killer before someone else is murdered with connections to Bronner Pharmaceuticals.

Faye M. Benjamin

CHAPTER 1

In the corporate world of business, there exists an imaginary corporate ladder to the top. The steps of this ladder resemble a battlefield littered with broken spirits, lost dreams, and shattered people. Why do some people stomp up that ladder crushing other employees under their feet to get to the top? Is this corporate battlefield caused by greed, money, power, and jealousy, or is it simpler than that? Is it really the good versus the evil in mankind's souls?

A person has stalked Dr. Duane Newby, deputy CEO of Bronner Pharmaceuticals, for several weeks to find out his routine and where best to kill him. This four day medical conference might provide the perfect opportunity to eliminate the hated doctor.

Dr. Newby was attending a four day conference in August, 2009 in Washington, D. C. When the meetings were over, several members went out to dinner before returning to their hotel rooms. Newby went back to his room and turned on the news. The weather report alarmed him, because it was calling for severe thunderstorms and damaging winds. He called his wife to let her know he was on his way home, because he wanted to get home before the storms hit. Duane knew his wife didn't react well to storms and power outages, so he threw his suitcase and briefcase in the car and started home.

The skies kept getting darker, and the wind was whipping the trees. Thunder boomed in the distance, and lightning flashed across the angry sky. He prayed he could beat the storm before the worst hit. Within a heartbeat, the sky turned black, the rain came down in torrents, and the violent wind rocked his car.

As the rain poured outside, Dr. Newby strained to see the road. His windshield wipers were on high, but they couldn't seem to keep up with the pelting rain. He felt like he was driving through a thick fog when he noticed headlights in his rearview mirror. Those headlights kept getting bigger until Duane shouted, "Get off my bumper, you idiot! I can't see, so I'm not going any faster!"

Suddenly, the vehicle behind him turned on its high beams blinding him, and the vehicle rammed into the back of his car as Duane fought to keep his car on the road. Duane drove faster trying to get away from this maniac, but the vehicle bumped him again. Within seconds, he slid off the road, down an embankment, and into a thick stand of trees. A huge tree limb crashed through the windshield, and crushed Duane against the seat.

As his life's blood drained from his body, a person outside the car laughed and said, *"You were an arrogant prick, and it was time to get rid of you. You stomped on a lot of people climbing that corporate ladder, you piece of crap. Well guess what, Duane; you just fell off the ladder. I didn't even have to finish you off; Mother Nature took real good care of you."*

Dr. Newby's funeral was full of tears, sadness, and disbelief. The owner and CEO of Bronner Pharmaceuticals, Dr. Kurt Bronner, tried his best to console his grieving widow. How many tears shed at the funeral were actually tears of joy? How much laughter was hidden behind those sad faces? How many people left the cemetery saying, "Goodbye, you prick?"

A month after Dr. Newby's death, Dr. Bronner hired a very close college friend of his to become the new deputy CEO. Dr. Bronner convinced his friend to leave California and come live in Virginia. He made the deal even sweeter by offering Dr. Michael Lim a twenty-thousand dollar pay raise, a ten-thousand dollar signing bonus, and part ownership in the business.

Dr. Bronner called several meetings to introduce the company's new deputy CEO. Dr. Lim was impressed with the research and testing departments and was looking forward to working with top notch scientists.

In an office behind closed doors, a person thinks, *"I can't believe Dr. Bronner hired this idiot outside the company all the way from the West Coast. Why didn't he promote someone right here who is well qualified for the position? The man is making a lot more money a year than Newby was making, so what kind of crap is that? I got rid of that prick, Newby, but it looks like I'll have to get rid of some more."*

Timmy Bronner's mom picked him up from Stargate Academy and drove home while he told her how his day went at school. When they got home, Timmy asked if he could play in his tree house. His mother told him yes, but reminded him to change clothes first. He ran out the patio doors, because he wanted to play with his friend, Becky (his spirit friend). He climbed the tree house ladder and waited for her to appear.

He said, "There you are. I've been waiting for you, Becky."

"I have a big surprise for you, Timmy."

"I love your surprises, because they're a lot of fun."

"Remember me telling you about the 3M ladies, Dolly, Art, Mandy, and Adam?"

"Sure, I do."

"You have to do something very important, right now. You must follow me to get help for your family, because they are in danger."

"What's wrong?"

"Hurry, they are in bad danger! We have to get them help, now! We have to go this way to get away from the bad person!"

Timmy scrambled down the ladder and raced after Becky. She was taking him deeper into the woods and far away from his house. "Why is my family in danger?" He tried to be careful, but several times he stumbled and fell. Becky waited for him to get up and kept encouraging him to follow her to get help.

"Becky, why can't I run back home to help them?"

"We have to go this way."

He stumbled again, ripped his jeans, and cut his knee. He was breathing hard, and couldn't get up, so Becky stayed by him and told him to rest for a little while. After several minutes had passed, Becky got Timmy up to follow her to Millie's farmhouse. Even though he was tired, thirsty, and his knee hurt, Timmy kept following Becky wondering how far he had to walk to get help.

In mid-November, a person disabled the Bronner security system and broke into the house around 3:30 pm. The mother and daughter were herded into the kitchen, made to lie on the floor, and then shot in the back of the head.

The house was trashed and certain things were stolen while the evil person tore the house apart trying to find the kid. The outside, shed, garage, and the woods behind the house were checked. *"Where the hades is the kid?"*

Tears started rolling down Timmy's face, because he was afraid and hurt all over.

"Don't cry, because we're almost there. Be real brave Timmy, because these people will hide and protect you. Remember, I came to save you."

Becky led him pass a cabin onto a path leading out of the woods. When he reached the tree line, Becky said, "Walk to the house, and you will be safe."

While Mabel, Mandy (two of the three ladies who run Freestone's safe house network), and Sierra (Freestone's receptionist) started preparing dinner, Dolly and Art Hamilton (Freestone's Director and Financial Advisor) went outside on the deck to enjoy the mild weather. They were holding each other close and laughing, when Dolly noticed movement at the tree line to Millie's cabin.

"Did you see that, Art?"

"See what, Lady Bug?"

"Down by the tree line. My Lord, it's a little boy stumbling out of the trees coming towards us!"

Art ordered, "Dolly, get Dan (Freestone's Deputy Director), Cody (Freestone investigative agent), and Millie (third lady who runs Freestone's safe house network and Dan's mother) out here, quickly! I'll head for the boy."

All five adults rushed down towards the little boy who

dropped to the ground exhausted, dirty, hungry, and thirsty. Poor Timmy was frightened out of his wits and just couldn't take another step.

Art reached Timmy first right after the boy collapsed and said, "Don't be afraid, I'll keep you safe. What's your name?"

Breathing heavily, the boy struggled to say, "Timmy. Please hide and keep me safe. My mommy, daddy, and sissy need help! Are you Mr. Art?"

"Yes, but how do you know my name?"

"Becky told me you would help me. I'm scared!"

"Why does your family need help?"

"Becky told me they were in bad danger, and she made me follow her through the woods to get here, forever!"

If Art had false teeth, they would have dropped out of his mouth from shock. He knew Millie, Vince, and Kris talked to this Becky, but now this. He didn't understand this gift of sight and Becky, but if this boy got here because of her, then it had to be true. All the rest of the group got to Timmy and dropped on their knees around him. Millie went into her nurse mode and asked, "Are you hurt, little feller?"

"My knee hurts, and I can't walk through the woods anymore. Are you Ms. Millie?"

The whole group could have been knocked over by a feather. Millie asked, "How do you know my name?"

"Becky told me about you, and you got to help my mommy, daddy, and sissy!"

Timmy started to cry, so Art picked him up in his arms and headed for the house. Art asked him what his last name was, where he lived, and told him they would get help for his family. When the group got to the house, Millie started cleaning up his knee, put medicine on it, and bandaged it up. She wiped his face and hands, then gave him some water to drink and a banana. Poor Timmy gobbled down the banana then dropped off to sleep from pure exhaustion.

Adam (recovering Freestone security agent) said, "I'll hold him while you folks decide what to do. Look at his tennis shoes, they're trashed."

Art said, "If Becky brought him here and told this precious child his family was in danger, then we better find out what's wrong."

Sheridan (serial killer survivor recovering at Millie's safe house) spoke up and said, "A little girl named Becky helped me get away from that monster, and helped Vince find me."

Millie asked, "Do you remember anything about her?"

She answered, "Yes, she had light brown hair; dressed kind of old fashioned, and carried an orange cat in her arms."

Millie replied in shock, "Well, I'll be darn; that's our Becky. So, Millie explained her meetings with Becky."

Dolly replied, "We don't say a word about this boy until we know what's going on. I'm going to call Vince, so Dan and I can talk this over with him."

Supervisor Vince Chappell (head of investigative teams at Freestone) was getting ready to leave for the day when a picture flashed in his mind. He saw a man, woman, and a girl lying on the floor shot in the head. "What good is this picture if I don't know where it is?" Just then, he got a call from Dolly telling him what happened, and he told her about the picture he saw before her call. Those three people he saw had to be Timmy's family, so he told Dolly he'd get Chad busy putting a security detail together.

Ruth Parrish got into her car with a cake she baked for Greta and Timmy. She pulled up to the house, got out of the car with the cake, and walked up to the front door. Suddenly, she stopped when she saw the front door open. She edged a little closer and saw Dr. Bronner's body lying in a pool of blood. The poor woman dropped the cake, burst into tears, and fumbled for her cell phone in her purse. As she called 911, she ran back to her car and locked herself inside.

When the police arrived, the poor seventy-five year old woman was a basket case. Finally, she got composed enough to tell the police she saw Dr. Bronner's body on the floor.

When Detective Gage got to the house and went inside, he was stunned. The house was ransacked, Dr. Bronner was dead on the living room floor, and Mrs. Bronner and the daughter were dead on the kitchen floor shot in the head.

One officer saw a boy's bedroom, searched it, and searched the surrounding area. He told Gage he couldn't find the boy in the house, shed, or garage. The police asked the neighbor if she knew where the son was, but she told them she had no idea. Gage called for more officers to widen the search for the boy. "Was he dead somewhere else, or was he kidnapped?" God, he hoped they could find him alive. Right now, all he had were three dead family members and their missing son.

Dolly called Detective Gage and asked, "Are you busy right now, Bill?"

"Yes, I'm at a gruesome crime scene with three dead and a missing boy."

"Bill, Timmy Bronner wandered up to Millie's farmhouse about 4:45 pm exhausted and scared out of his wits. He said his family needed help and begged us to hide him."

"Is the boy hurt?"

"He has a cut up knee from stumbling around in the woods."

"Did he see the murder?"

"No, he says Becky led him away from the house to get help."

"Is this Vince's Becky?"

"Yes, it is, and she saved this boy's life. I know what you're thinking, but just try to keep an open mind like I'm trying to do. I don't believe in supernatural hocus pocus, but I can't argue with the results."

"Sweet Jesus Dolly, here we go, again."

"I'm putting Timmy under Freestone protection. Vince and Chad (head of Freestone's security-surveillance department) are putting together a security detail around the clock at Millie's farmhouse."

"I agree. I've already issued an Amber Alert, so let's keep that in place. As far as the media and the public are concerned, the boy is missing."

"Bill, the killer already knows the boy wasn't at home, so let's keep the killer guessing."

"I won't be able to talk with the boy today or tomorrow. I'll get back with you to set something up. Dolly, I'm so glad you have him, because I know you'll keep him safe."

"Thanks Bill, I'll talk to you later."

While Timmy slept in Adam's arms, Dolly addressed the group saying, "Timmy's family was murdered execution style, and there is no doubt in my mind this little boy is in serious danger, so I'm putting him under Freestone protection. No one else needs to know we have him, because his life depends on our silence. He needs to be around people who will love and protect him. In my opinion, there's power behind this execution, not a robbery.

Supervisor Chad Napier (head of Freestone's security-surveillance department) is putting together a detail for around the clock protection here. Millie, let's keep Timmy here, not in the cabin. That way the agents can use the cabin to sleep in."

Cody spoke up and said, "I know I'm on down time, but I

want to stay here."

"Alright Cody, when the detail gets here, go home and pack what you need. You can come back tonight or in the morning."

Dolly continued, "Tomorrow, when we know more about this situation, Art and I plan to meet with Judge Franklin, so we can get custody of Timmy."

Mabel spoke up and said, "When he wakes up, we'll get some good food into him and introduce him to Pixie and Dixie who have already switched over to guard dog mode. Just look at those two flea bags around the chair Adam is sitting in."

Pixie and Dixie looked at each other and thought, "Don't worry folks, we'll keep him safe, because we're on guard duty. In other words, it's show time people, and we're on the case!"

Sierra added, "Timmy will need some clothes and shoes."

Art jumped in and said, "You're right, so here's some money and if you need more let me know."

Adam added, "Don't forget a teddy bear, toys, coloring books, and crayons."

Sierra left on her mission to spend Art's money to fix this precious little boy up with clothes and lots of goodies.

Adam got Millie's attention and asked, "Could you set up a cot in my room, so he can sleep with me? Cody can sleep in the other bed. That way two of us can look after him, plus I know the dogs won't let him out of their sight."

"Of course, I was thinking about that, too."

Millie and Mandy went upstairs to set up the cot in Adam's room. When they finished, Becky appeared in the room. Millie saw her, smiled, and said, "Thank you for bringing little Timmy to us, and we'll keep him safe."

Mandy followed Millie's eyes, but only saw a fine mist. Even when Millie talked to the mist, she still couldn't see this Becky.

Becky said, "He is in danger; you must protect him. Mandy looks like his mother. She and Adam will love him and will become his new family."

Millie looked at Mandy and asked, "Did you see and hear Becky?"

"I'm sorry Millie; all I saw was a fine mist."

"She said you look like Timmy's mother, and that you will love him as your own."

Mandy laughed and said, "I didn't see him awake, but who wouldn't love such a precious child. He has the cutest blonde wavy hair and handsome face."

Millie added, "Did you notice how Adam was holding him in his arms?"

"Oh yes, and Adam has such a loving look on his face, too. Millie, how are we going to tell this angelic boy his parents and sister were murdered?"

"I don't know yet, but somehow we'll know when the time is right."

The security detail arrived at Millie's farmhouse, got settled in the cabin, and the first shift took up their positions. Mabel made sure the guys at the cabin got a good dinner before they went to sleep.

Cody drove home to pack, run a few errands, and decided to get a good night's sleep at home. Tomorrow, he would head back to Millie's place to join the detail, because he wanted to make sure Timmy and Sheridan were protected.

CHAPTER 2

Slowly, Timmy opened his eyes and sat up. He looked at Adam's smiling face and somehow knew he was safe.

The boy said, "You must be Adam, because your arm has a cast on it. Becky told me you got hurt at work, and the ladies are helping you get better."

"You're right. The ladies are taking real good care of me, and we're going to take good care of you and keep you safe. How is your knee, Timbo? Do you mind if I call you, Timbo?"

Timmy laughed and answered, "I like Timbo, and my knee hurts just a little bit."

"Are you hungry, Timbo?"

"I'm really hungry, Adam."

Art noticed Timmy was awake, so he went over to him and gave the little boy a big hug along with Millie who checked his knee.

She asked, "Does your knee feel better?"

"It feels better after you fixed it. He pointed to Erika (stalker survivor recovering at Millie's safe house) and asked, "Are you helping her get better?"

Erika replied, "I'm feeling much better, because the 3M ladies are taking real good care of me. By the way, my name is Erika."

Timmy asked, "What happened to you?"

"A bad man broke my leg, but the police caught him, so he won't be able to hurt me again."

"I'm glad." Timmy looked at Sheridan and asked, "Did a bad man hurt you?"

"He sure did, but the police caught him, so he won't bother me again. My name is Sheridan. Don't you worry one bit Timmy, because we'll keep you safe."

While Timmy was in Art's arms, he looked down at Pixie and Dixie around Art's feet. He laughed as Art put him down on the floor. The two dogs played with Timmy as he giggled and rolled around on the floor.

The dogs thought, "Don't worry Timbo; the bad people won't hurt you. We are on the case, little feller."

Timmy petted the dogs, played with them, and laughed like crazy. Dolly joined the crowd in the family room as they watched Pixie and Dixie do their thing for Timmy. She was so glad the dogs brought joy to this precious little boy.

The boy looked up at Dolly and said, "I like dogs, Ms. Dolly. They are a lot of fun and good pals." Suddenly, he stopped and said, "I got to pee pee. Where is the bathroom?"

Adam took his hand and showed him where the bathroom was, laughing the whole way. Everyone laughed at the way he crunched up his nose when he said he had to pee.

Sierra returned from her shopping spree while Timmy was in the bathroom. Art and Dolly helped her bring in the bags loaded with all kinds of things. Of course, the most important of all was the teddy bear, little football, and a fire truck. She did what Art said, because the only change she gave Art back was $2.03. Dolly busted out laughing when Sierra put the money in Art's hand. Dolly said, "Sierra, you're my kind of woman when it comes to shopping."

Mabel and Mandy walked into the family room while everyone was looking at all the clothes and toys Sierra bought for Timmy. Mandy picked up the teddy bear and said, "It's so cute. I drug around a teddy bear when I was a kid."

Adam and Timmy walked down the hall into the family room. When Timmy saw Mandy, he ran to her, and launched himself around her legs. She picked him up into her arms and hugged him as he began to sob big crocodile tears. She stroked his hair and kept telling him they would keep him safe. She told him how brave he was, and that Becky was proud of him. She told him Pixie and Dixie would protect him and be his new playmates. She continued to stroke his hair, kiss his cheek, and wipe his tears away.

Adam looked into Mandy's eyes and knew this little boy was their destiny. Finally, he realized he loved Mandy with all his heart and wanted to spend the rest of his life with her. He didn't want to be a lonely old bachelor. He wanted to protect Mandy, and this precious little boy from all the evil people.

Mabel swallowed a knot in her throat as tears rolled down her cheeks along with everybody else. Watching a precious child crying tore Mabel up and ripped her heart out.

Adam walked up to Mandy and Timmy and hugged them both, tenderly. Timmy raised his head, looked at Mandy, and asked, "My mommy, daddy, and sissy are in heaven aren't they?"

Mandy kissed his forehead, looked into his tear-filled eyes, and answered, "Yes, they're in heaven, but don't be afraid, because we will love and protect you. Don't ever forget that your mommy, daddy, and sissy will always be in your thoughts and heart. They know Becky saved you by bringing you here. The police will find the person who did this and put them in jail, forever. Now, look at this cute teddy bear Sierra got for you."

Timmy hugged it and laid his head on Mandy's shoulder. Mabel came over and patted his back and asked, "Do you like spaghetti, Timbo?"

He looked at Mabel, smiled, and said, "Yes, ma'am."

Mabel said, "I make fantastic spaghetti with little meatballs, garden salads, and I can bake lots of delicious desserts. Do you like Red Velvet cake, Timbo?"

"I don't know what a Red Velvet cake is."

Dan added, "You'll have to try some to see if you like it, because it's my favorite."

"Are you Mabel?"

"I sure am, honey child."

"Becky told me you were a great cook, real funny, and you wear great big, crazy hats."

Mabel replied, "Becky is right. I have lots of crazy hats and crazy earrings."

"Can I see one, Ms. Mabel?'

Mabel scooted upstairs, put on her most outrageous hat, and proudly walked into the family room to model her hat. Instantly, Timmy's tears and sobs turned to giggles and laughter from his toes up as he watched Mabel model her hat. The entire group laughed and clapped as Mabel made one curtsey after another. She walked up to Timmy and asked, "May I have this dance, Mr. Timmy?"

He laughed as Mandy slipped him into Mabel's arms. She hummed a waltz as she whirled the little boy around the floor while they both giggled like a bunch of monkeys at a banana bar. Finally, Mabel put him down and curtsied in front of him. Adam whispered in his ear to give Ms. Mabel a true southern gentleman's bow.

Mabel said, "Now, Mr. Timmy, come and help Mandy and me set the table for dinner, because I bet you are very hungry." She took his little hand, and the three of them headed for the kitchen as Mandy gave him his teddy bear.

Art looked at Dolly and said, "I don't believe what I just saw. Mandy treated him like he was her own son. Mabel just showed me a side of her I didn't know existed. Adam, I see you've taken to that little fellow in a special way."

Adam answered, "I'd die protecting that boy."

Art spoke up and said, "If I have to spend every dime of my money to keep him safe, I'll do it."

Adam added, "Millie, I will never make fun of you two ladies' crazy hats, crazy earrings, and power purses, again."

Dolly piped in, "Now Adam, you know how important love and laughter are in people's lives, especially the children."

Dan asked, "Mom, how far did that little feller walk to get here?"

"I think about a mile and a half across heavily wooded countryside."

Sheridan replied, "Sweet Jesus, bless his little heart. No wonder his tennis shoes are a mess."

Timmy helped Mabel and Mandy set the table for dinner. He was so hungry he couldn't wait to dive into the salad, spaghetti, and garlic bread. He kept looking at the Red Velvet cake wondering what it tasted like. When he thought nobody was looking, he stuck his little finger in the icing. He didn't know what kind of icing it was, but it sure tasted good.

Mandy showed him where the dogs ate and asked him to help her put food and water down for them. Pixie and Dixie gobbled down their food and water like they hadn't eaten in a week. Timmy crunched up his nose and pointed his little finger at them and said, "Don't eat so fast! It'll give you a stomach ache, or you might choke and throw up on the floor."

Mabel and Mandy couldn't help but laugh at the way the dogs looked at him. Both of the dogs wondered how Timbo would react to Greedy Gut, and the rest of Millie's wild kingdom.

Everyone gathered around the table, and Mandy made sure Timbo sat next to her and Adam. As Millie stood up to say the blessing, Timmy noticed everybody was holding hands, so he grabbed Mandy and Adam's hands. Mandy looked at him and winked, as he rewarded her with a megawatt smile. Everyone pigged out including Timmy who looked around the table and said, "I liked the spaghetti and salad."

Dolly said, "Tell us what foods you don't like."

He crunched up his nose and said, "I don't like liver, boney fish, and hot peppers."

Dan asked, "What are your favorite fruits?"

"I love all fruits, but I hate apricots."

Sierra asked, "What are your favorite movies?"

"I love Davy Crockett, Daniel Boone, Harry Potter, Pirates of the Caribbean, and history movies."

The folks at the table looked at each other like Timmy had three heads, suddenly.

Erika asked, "What are your favorite TV shows?"

"I love Little House on the Prairie, the Waltons, the Disney Channel, Discovery Channel, History Channel, and all quiz shows."

Now, the folks at the table were convinced Timbo had five heads.

Sheridan asked, "What is your all-time favorite movie you could watch over and over again?"

"I love the Sound of Music, Oliver, and Star Wars."

Art shook his head and asked, "Are you sure you are five years old?"

"Yes sir, I'm five years old, but my birthday is December 5th, then I'll be six years old."

Mandy spoke up and said, "Well, that means Mabel and I will have to bake you a big birthday cake and have a big party for you."

Timbo clapped his hands and giggled, then asked, "When can we eat the Red Velvet cake?"

Mabel replied, "We can eat it as soon as I can slice it."

Art asked him, "Where do you go to school?"

"I go to Stargate Academy, sir."

Everyone laughed as the ladies cleared the table, and got the sheet cake ready to slice. Mabel did the honors, and gave Timbo the first slice. With icing on his lips, he smiled and said, "This is the best cake in the whole world."

Sheridan and Sierra had to agree, because they never tasted a Red Velvet cake, either.

Needless to say, there was only a few crumbs left of the cake, so Timbo finished them off with a big grin on his face. The 3M ladies and Sierra cleaned up the kitchen while the others got comfortable in the family room. Erika was getting around much better, so she didn't need as much help as Sheridan. Timmy noticed a piano in one corner of the family room, and asked Adam who played it. He told the boy that Millie and Mabel played it quite often when they wanted to relax. The little feller went into the kitchen and asked Millie if he could play the piano. Millie told him he could as long as he didn't bang on the keys.

He crawled up on the bench, got settled, and started playing. While washing the dishes, Mandy looked at Mabel and asked, "Do you hear that beautiful music? Who's playing the piano?"

Millie replied, "Timmy asked me if he could play it, but that can't be him."

All the ladies walked into the family room and were shocked to stone. Mabel said, "My Lord, he's playing Disney theme songs and love songs I recognize. Sweet Jesus, this boy is no average five year old."

As Timmy played his favorite songs, everyone sat around the piano for the next twenty-five minutes spellbound. When he finished, everybody applauded and told him how wonderful his music made them feel.

Mandy gathered him in her arms, kissed him, and told him

how special his music was. He said, "I wanted to make everybody happy, but you are crying."

She answered, 'They aren't sad tears, but happy tears, my little man."

While Sierra and Adam showed Timmy his new toys and clothes in the family room, Dolly, Art, Dan, and the 3M ladies slipped into the kitchen to talk privately.

Art added, "The sick lowlife who murdered his family can never know the boy is here."

Millie said, "This boy does not have the mind of a normal five year old. In my opinion, he's extremely gifted like Heather. He could be a child prodigy."

Art asked Dolly, "Is there any way we can get into the house to get all his things?"

She answered, "Oh yes, the police can get a search warrant. Since the entire family was murdered, the police will need to look for financial records, insurance documents, a will, and any other pertinent information."

Millie asked, "What happens to the bodies?"

Dolly replied, "I'm sure Chief Ramsey will have his medical examiner perform their autopsies at Freestone."

Dan added, "There is no way this little boy can go to their funerals."

Millie had such a sad look on her face when she said, "The

holidays are just around the corner, and this poor lad has lost everything."

Dolly took Millie's hand and said, "Look at me, Millie. He has lost one world, but he has inherited another fantastic world full of crazy people."

Art chimed in and said, "He's going to have lots of crazy new relatives."

Dolly told Millie they had to leave, so she could call Chief Ramsey and Detective Gage. Tomorrow, Art and she were going to Freestone to meet with Vince and Dan, so they could decide how to handle Timmy's situation. When she had the information she needed from the whiz kids, then she and Art would meet with Judge Franklin.

They said their goodbyes to everyone, and both of them gave Timmy a big hug and kiss. Sierra said her goodbyes, and hugged her sister and Timbo. The little feller gave her lots of kisses and hugs for getting all the clothes and toys for him. Dan said his goodbyes, hugged Timbo and his mother, then kissed Erika's forehead.

Millie wondered, "What's this? My son just kissed a woman, affectionately, for the first time since his nasty divorce from a true witch seven years ago. It's about time you opened up your heart, son."

Mandy looked at Timmy and said, "I think you need a warm soapy bath and your hair washed, Mr. Timbo. Then, you can wear a pair of your new pajamas and slippers."

"Will you help me take my bath?'

"Sure, if you want me to."

"What about my knee?"

Millie replied, "I'll put a new bandage on it when you finish your bath, sweetheart."

Mandy carried him upstairs for his bath while Mabel and Adam brought up the bags of clothes, and his new teddy bear.

Adam decided to get his shower, so he could watch over Timbo when the little feller fell asleep. There were Freestone agents in the house, but Timmy would be in Adam's room on the cot. If he could help it, no one was going to get to this boy.

Erika looked at Millie and said, "You must feel like you're running a flea bag motel around here. We sure are one sorry bunch who can't even help you."

"Ah, I won't have it any other way, so have you ladies noticed the fireworks going off between Adam and Mandy?'

Erika laughed and answered, "I'm surprised the house hasn't burned down, because I keep waiting for Adam's hair to catch fire."

All the ladies laughed like hyenas while Millie brought in some oatmeal cookies for them to snack on. As they munched on their cookies, Lottie, the night nurse (hired by Freestone), buzzed Millie to let her in.

Millie introduced Nurse Lottie to Sheridan and proceeded to tell the nurse about Timmy and how important her silence was concerning the boy.

Lottie said in disbelief, "Why Ms. Millie, none of us will be flapping our jaws about this to nobody! Lucy, Isa, and I love you folks, and we wouldn't do anything to hurt you. If somebody tries to hurt any of you, I'll kick them in the nuts and yank their hair out before they can pee in their pants, honey child. They don't call us specialized, private nurses for nothing. Why, we go way back taking care of the people Mr. Art loves, so you can count on us, Ms. Millie."

Millie replied, "You ladies are the best."

Adam came down to the family room after his shower and welcomed Lottie with a hug. He told the group there was a lot of giggling coming from Mandy's bathroom. He got comfortable in a chair grabbed some oatmeal cookies to munch on, and Millie brought him a glass of milk.

Mandy brought Timmy down to the family room all clean and smelling real good. Millie introduced Lottie and told him why she was here.

The little feller asked, "Are you going to take care of my hurt knee, Ms. Lottie?"

"Of course, I will you sweet thing. You look mighty handsome in your Scooby-Doo pajamas and slippers."

"I really like them."

Lottie put medicine on his knee and put a new bandage on it.

Millie got Timmy some cookies and a glass of milk, so Mandy could go back upstairs to get her bath. Timbo crawled up in Adam's lap and hugged his neck.

Adam thought, "Sweet Jesus, I wish you were mine."

Lottie took Sheridan to her suite to tackle her bath and night routine. When she finished with Sheridan, she would get Erika all set for bedtime.

Mabel came down after her bath wearing an outrageous pair of bunny rabbit slippers with big floppy ears. Timmy squealed and giggled like crazy every time he looked at them. Of course, Mabel went through her modeling routine, so the little tike would get the full affect. Mabel put on a Disney movie, so everyone could enjoy it right along with Timbo. It wasn't long before the little feller was fast asleep in Adam's lap. Carefully, Adam took him upstairs to his room and put him on the cot with his teddy bear. Adam crawled into bed and thought, "I promise to love and protect him." As Adam drifted off to sleep, this tragic, sad day, but somehow joyful day came to an end.

CHAPTER 3

When Dolly and Art arrived at home, she put in a call to Chief Ramsey and Detective Gage for an update. She learned that Dr. Bronner's company was in Stafford County which meant two counties would be involved in this case.

Chief Ramsey asked Dolly if Freestone would be willing to host a joint task force to investigate this bizarre murder. Of course, Dolly said Freestone would help both counties in any way they could. Chief Ramsey and Gage agreed Timmy Bronner needed to be in protective custody under Dolly's care. Chief Ramsey and Sheriff Patterson from Stafford County already agreed to assign Detectives Gage and Hansen to work with Freestone.

Dolly agreed to assign some Freestone agents to assist Gage and Hansen with the investigation.

While executing their search warrants, Chief Ramsey agreed to box up all of Timmy's belongings and send them to Freestone along with the evidence and the victims. Of course, the county medical examiner was more than happy to use Freestone's autopsy suite.

Dolly assured the Chief her whiz kids would dig up every fact involving the family, and Dr. Bronner's company, as soon as possible.

Once Dolly finished talking with the Chief, she called Vince to fill him in on all the events. Her next call went to Walt Hensley (Art's best friend and security guru) asking him to meet them at Freestone the next day to discuss the security plan for Freestone's safe house network. That plan needed to be put in motion as soon as possible. She wanted Millie's farmhouse, and the stone farmhouse property done first. She didn't want another breach in security at either property.

Art shook his head at how easily Dolly could wheel and deal right up there with the best of them. He thought Walt and he were master wheeler-dealers, but Dolly was a master at it, too.

Art fell back on his pillow an exhausted pile of flesh after making mad, passionate love to his wonderful wife. Sex had never been this good for him, and Dolly was one sexy bombshell, in his opinion. This woman made him weak in the knees just looking at her. Finally, he found his piece of paradise in his wife's arms.

As the contented couple drifted off to sleep, they knew tomorrow would be a very busy day at Freestone. At least, they knew little Timmy was safe and surrounded by a lot of loving people to protect him, as well as Pixie and Dixie.

The next morning was Thursday, November 19, 2009 Freestone employees got to work early to tackle a difficult day.

Deputy Director Dan Kramer met with Freestone's whiz kids, Shontelle Davis and Jason Hartman, and told them he wanted all the information they could find on Dr. Kurt Bronner, his family, and Bronner Pharmaceuticals.

Meanwhile, Dr. Heather Burfoot (Freestone's forensic scientist) and her department were busy processing the Bronner evidence they received, so far. The medical examiner from Prince William County was performing the autopsies on Dr. Bronner, Mrs. Bronner, and Greta Bronner. Heather performed her usual brief ceremony concerning the victims. She lightly touched each victim with a dove's feather, and prayed their souls would find peace. It crushed Heather's heart to watch an autopsy on children like Greta.

Vince called Byron Sawyer and Team 7 into his office to prepare them for Freestone's next task force. Byron was very familiar with joint task forces, because he worked with Detective Gage and Detective Hansen on Task Force Greene that caught serial killers Andrew Logan and Nicole Fowler. He worked with Hansen on Task Force Curtain to catch serial killer Lonnie Baldwin before he could murder his last hostage.

Team 7 successfully concluded their Justice Department case, and enjoyed their week of down time. Both men were eager to tackle this case, because it required a joint task force between Freestone, Stafford, and Prince William Counties.

Vince looked at his three investigative agents and said, "This case involves the murder of Dr. Kurt Bronner and his family. Bronner is the owner and CEO of Bronner Pharmaceuticals in Stafford County north of Dodd's Corner. Three family members were murdered in their home off

Aden Road in Nokesville, and their four year old son is missing."

"The whiz kids have compiled numerous printouts giving us information about the family and the business. Each of you has a packet to work from, and Detective Gage is bringing all the information he has from the crime scene.

As far as you know, the boy is missing. At this point in the investigation, you don't need to know anything about the boy. Does everyone understand what I mean?"

All three agents replied, "Yes, sir."

"Good. Now, go down to the task force conference room, digest those packets, so you are up to speed when Gage and Hansen get here."

When the agents left, Vince called Jason to his office. "Jason, I want you to find out all you can about Stargate Academy in Manassas that Timmy attended and bring it to me. Absolutely, no one is to know about this but you and me. Do you understand me, Jason?"

"Yes sir, you can trust me."

After Jason left, Gage and Hansen walked into Vince's office. They shook hands and sat around Vince's desk.

Gage commented, "Here we go again, Vince. I have a feeling this case will turn into another Pandora's Box full of nasty goodies, but this time we're starting from the beginning."

"A lot of Pandora's Boxes have fallen on our door steps, lately."

Hansen added, "Right now, we have three dead family members and no suspects. When we start studying your whiz kid's printouts, we should be able to start putting the puzzle together."

Gage spoke up, "Yep, the puzzle will be one of those thousand pieces jobs. So, who do you have to join the task force?"

Vince replied, "Since you really like Byron Sawyer's investigative skills, I've assigned him to the task force, and Team 7 is ready to help you. Cody is staying with the protection detail, so when Travis gets back from his down time you can have him. Are these four okay with you?"

Gage replied, "All four are fantastic! I'm more than pleased with the help Freestone makes available to us."

"Thanks a lot for telling me that. Let's call this case Task Force Bronner. Anyone have an idea for a code name for the killer?"

Hansen chimed in, "How about Cobra, because this killer is like a deadly snake."

"Okay, that works for me."

Hansen looked at Vince and added, "If you have useful tips please tell us, because you made a believer out of me on the last task force."

Vince answered, "I'll let you know, but I might not see or

hear anything. This gift drives me crazy, sometimes."

Vince handed Gage and Hansen packets filled with printouts from the whiz kids, they shook hands, and the detectives headed to the conference room to join the other three agents.

Jason walked into Vince's office and gave him the printouts on Stargate Academy and Timothy Bronner. He said, "I don't know what you think, but this kid is right up there with Heather. The school had him listed as a child prodigy when he was enrolled a year ago. That's some heavy duty brains, and he has a photographic memory, Boss."

"In other words, you're telling me we're brain dead compared to him."

"Boss, our brains are torched extra crispy."

"Lord, that's downright scary, Jason."

"You bet! Well, I'm off to my trusty computer, so I can get the task force more information."

The next day Art, Dolly, Dan, and Vince met in a conference room at 10:30 am to discuss Stargate Academy and a general overview of the case.

Vince looked at Art and Dolly and said, "This is what we have so far on Timmy's family. Kurt Bronner and his maternal grandparents escaped from East Berlin, but during that escape, Kurt's parents and paternal grandparents were killed. The family immigrated to the United States and later became naturalized citizens. The maternal grandparents died in the early 1990's.

Mrs. Bronner spent five years in foster care after her parents overdosed on drugs. Her paternal grandmother drowned when Mrs. Bronner was eight, and her maternal grandparents were killed in a car accident while driving drunk. Her last foster care parents put her through a two year business school and helped her get a decent job. Dr. Bronner and his wife were married twelve years ago.

Art asked, "You mean this little boy doesn't have any living relatives?"

"That's right, Art."

Dolly added, "My Lord, that's awful. That boy will not go into foster care if I have to adopt him myself."

Vince said, "There is a reason why Becky led him to Millie's place, and I bet you it involves our Freestone family in some way."

"Okay, here is what we have on Stargate Academy. Timmy was enrolled there a year ago as a child prodigy. Currently, he is doing the equivalent of tenth grade work. He has a photographic memory, plays the piano, speaks German, and is quite computer savvy."

Art added, "He can't go back to that school, because he's in danger. I think we should get a private tutor for him who is trustworthy. I can make some calls and see what I can come

35

up with."

Dolly replied, "He needs to get back on a routine with his schooling to keep his mind occupied."

Vince gave Dolly and Dan an overview of the case from the information, so far. Vince let them know Detective Gage brought the boxes from Timmy's room, and they could get them from Heather.

Dolly asked, "Have the police found a will, banking records, and insurance policies?"

"Yes, and Gage is working through all that, now."

Dolly added, "When Art and I meet with Judge Franklin, that information he'll need to know about. Timmy must stay hidden, but the court will have to protect the boy's interests according to the will."

After the four ate lunch at the Deli, Walt met them at Freestone to go over the security plan for the safe house network. Once Walt explained the entire plan to Art and Dolly, she asked several questions which were answered to her satisfaction.

Then she asked, "How soon can you finish Millie's property?"

Walt answered, "It should be completed a couple of weeks before Christmas."

"Good, get it done as soon as possible."

Walt added, "It's going to take a while to set the nerve center up at the stone farmhouse. Then, you'll need someone to get the nerve center put together and running smoothly."

Dolly jumped in and asked, "Walt, how would you like to become my Director of Safe House Security?"

Walt thought for a bit and said, "Alright, but under two conditions. First, I have plenty of money, so I don't need a salary. Second, let me hire two men I know who can handle the nerve center and train others to run it."

Dolly answered, ""Good, Art and you can handle this project and decide on salaries and personnel."

Art laughed and said, "Well Walt, it looks like I'm spending some more of our money."

Dolly chimed back, "Cricket, if you don't like it just say something. You know I'm having problems with your money becoming our money. Changing your will and your financial portfolio makes me feel like a gold digger, and I still can't believe your children went along with it."

Dan spoke up and said, "Dolly, Art told you he has already set up his children and grandchildren for life, so don't you dare feel guilty about the money. The money is helping and protecting people. That's what Freestone stands for."

The group said their goodbyes, so Art and Dolly could pick up Timmy's things and meet with Judge Franklin. The meeting with the judge went well, because Dolly knew him back when she was a lawyer for the Justice Department.

Millie and Dolly were given joint custody of Timmy, and he appointed Dolly Timmy's legal guardian and trustee of his estate. The judge agreed the boy needed to be in protective custody with Freestone, and the media told three family members were murdered, and the son is missing.

Judge Franklin told Dolly to come back on Monday with any legal documents found by the police. Dolly got permission to have Gage box up family pictures, photo albums, and family jewelry, so those things could be kept for the boy. As long as they weren't part of the evidence, Dolly was welcome to save those and anything else in the home or on the property for the boy. The judge knew the police and Freestone had a killer to catch, and a child to protect.

When Dolly and Art got home, she called Millie to let her know they would bring Timmy's belongings over on Friday.

After that Art made Dolly lie down and get some rest, because he knew she was tired. She wasn't a hundred percent yet after her surgery.

He got on the phone to see if he could arrange a tutor for Timmy, because the little boy needed to get back on a routine.

CHAPTER 4

Detectives Gage and Hansen joined the three agents in the conference room. Several easel boards were already set up for the group to use along with all the supplies they needed.

Gage started by saying, "We are starting this case from the beginning, because this is no cold case this time. Here are copies of the accident report involving the former Deputy CEO, Dr. Duane Newby. It was declared a fatal accident, because of the storm and slippery road conditions. Obviously, the tree limb killed Newby, but my gut tells me this was Cobra's first victim. Someone has removed the owner/CEO and deputy CEO, and we have to find out who and why."

Byron commented, "The photographs of the car show damage to the rear bumper, so he could have been forced off the road. I don't see anything in these reports about previous damage to the car, so I guess Mrs. Newby wasn't asked about that."

Gage looked at Byron and said, "I want you to talk to Mrs. Newby about the accident and ask her about the rear bumper."

Byron added, "He was returning from a business conference, so he should have had a cell phone and laptop with him. We should take a look at both of them, because there is nothing in the reports about them."

Hansen replied, "I agree with you and Gage. This fatal

accident wasn't caused by the weather. There's no coincidence here."

Gage continued, "Tomorrow, all of us are going to Bronner Pharmaceuticals and start interviewing the staff and employees. This is no robbery gone wrong, but a murder or hit, because someone wanted these two men dead. This smells like a possible case of corporate ladder murder; let me knock the top guys off, so I can move up the chain."

Hansen added, "Right now, everybody is a suspect including Dr. Michael Lim. Yes, he was in California when Newby died, and he was hired by Dr. Bronner. However, this could have been an ordered hit."

Gage moved to the first easel and wrote out Dr. Michael Lim. Ryan, what do we know so far about Lim?"

"He was a close college friend of Dr. Bronner's. In California, he was Deputy CEO of Richfield Pharmaceuticals in San Diego. He was hired after Dr. Newby was killed and is married with three children."

Gage moved to the next easel and wrote out Dr. Maxine Stine. Brad, what do we know about her?"

"She is Director of Research and has been with the company since its beginning. She is next in line behind the deputy CEO on the ladder and is divorced with no children."

Gage moved to the next easel and wrote Dr. Elwood Harris. Hansen, what do we know about him?"

"He is Director of Experimental Testing and has been with the company since the beginning. His position puts him behind Dr. Stine on the ladder and is married with four children."

Gage moved to the next easel and wrote Dr. Colin Zocrist. Byron, what do we know about him?"

"He is Director of Medical Production and has been with the company since the beginning. His position puts him behind Dr. Harris on the ladder; he's divorced with two children."

Gage moved to the next easel and divided it in half. Ryan, what do we know about Maria Santana?"

"She is Director of Contracts and has been with the company for three years. Her position doesn't put her on the corporate ladder, and she is single."

Gage asked, "Brad, what do we know about Dillon Carr?"

"He is Director of Finances and has been with the company since the beginning. His position is not part of the corporate ladder, and he is single."

Gage moved to the last easel and divided it in half. "Hansen, what do we know about Vernell Cleveland?"

"She is Director of IT and has been with the company for four years. She's not on the corporate ladder; she is married with three children."

Gage looked at Byron and asked, "What do we know about Hansa Fareed?"

"She is Dr. Bronner's secretary, has worked for him for three years, and she is single."

Gage continued, "We need to find out a lot more about all these people, because we have to circle the wagons closer and closer until Cobra pops out. Tomorrow, I'll talk with Dr. Lim and Dr. Zocrist.

"Hansen, you interview Dr. Stine and Vernell Cleveland."

"Ryan, you talk with Dr. Harris and Maria Santana. Brad, you interview the Director of Finance, Dillon Carr, the head of shipping and receiving, Jesse Rice, and the head of security, Harry Dent."

"Byron, you take the senior scientists in Research, Testing, Production, and Hansa Fareed, Dr. Bronner's secretary. Also, set up an appointment with Mrs. Newby."

Hansen remarked, "DEA will probably want to check the books to make sure no medicine is leaving this facility, illegally. We are requesting an audit to see if there are any money issues."

Ryan asked, "If someone asks about a funeral, what do we tell them?"

"Tell them we're in the process of notifying the next of kin, and we'll let them know when arrangements have been made."

Gage added, "Make sure you say three family members were murdered, and the son is missing."

Brad commented, "Maybe, Cobra isn't worried about the missing boy. At age five, the boy certainly isn't capable of running the company."

Ryan replied, "Cobra probably thinks Dr. Lim will become acting CEO, and that means someone becomes the deputy CEO. If I were Dr. Lim, I'd be looking over my shoulder figuring I'm next."

Byron remarked, "We sure are up to our necks in possible suspects."

Gage said, "Let's discuss the crime scene. Cobra disabled the alarm system to get inside. Mrs. Bronner and the daughter were lying face down on the kitchen floor when they were shot in the back of the head. Mrs. Bronner fought her attacker, because she had several broken fingernails and bruises on her arms and neck. The daughter had bruising on her arms and neck, too. Dr. Bronner was attacked and shot above the left temple in the living room near the front door."

"As you can tell from the photographs, the house was ransacked, and it appears Cobra did more destroying than stealing. For example, Mrs. Bronner's wallet still had money and credit cards in it, and her cell phone was still in her purse. Dr. Bronner's laptop and cell phone were still in his briefcase, and his wallet still had money and credit cards in it. The objective was murder, not robbery."

Hansen added, "All of them were shot with a twenty-two caliber handgun at close range. This was an up close and personal murder."

Ryan asked, "Did the neighbors hear or see anything useful?"

Gage replied, "The nearest neighbor is a half a mile away, and she didn't see or hear anything. A church friend found

Dr. Bronner's body and called 911 around 5:00 pm."

Brad asked, "Was Mrs. Bronner or her daughter sexually assaulted?"

"Heather's report says no. Holy Crap! Mrs. Bronner was five months pregnant."

Hansen remarked, "If Dr. Bronner isn't the father, then we have another needle in the haystack."

Byron commented, "We know next to nothing about this family, so we need to look at their private lives. Maybe, she was having an affair, or both were having affairs. We've got a lot of work to do to uncover the facts, so I guess we jump into the haystack and start looking for those needles."

Ryan remarked, "Now, we need to find out if Cobra was her lover and didn't want to be a daddy. Of course, Heather will run DNA on the fetus, and then we will know for sure."

Brad asked, "Gage, do we let the cat out of the bag and ask the employees if Dr. Bronner knew his wife was pregnant?"

"I say we stir the pot up good, so let's throw that out there and see what happens."

Gage looked at the task force and said, "We have a ton of interviews to conduct, because I want that entire work force at the company questioned. We have to peel back every layer until we get to Cobra."

Hansen remarked, "Jason is working on the financial status of the major players on the staff. If there's a red flag, Jason will find it. All of us know money turns a lot of people into monsters who will do anything to get it."

Byron added, "I think power, greed, and jealousy are driving Cobra, too."

Ryan remarked, "Yep, those evil issues are all tangled up in this case."

Gage continued, "According to Shontelle's printouts, none of our major players have been in serious trouble with the law. Dr. Harris has one speeding ticket, and Dr. Zocrist has a reckless driving ticket on his record."

Hansen remarked, "We need to make a visit to Stargate Academy where Timothy is enrolled. Maybe, the owner might know something useful about the family and its history. Ryan, you take that interview when you can work it in. Find out who was giving him piano lessons, but remember the family was killed, and the son is missing."

Gage continued, "Brad, I want you to go to Greta Bronner's school, and see if they have any useful information about the family."

Byron asked, "Do we know of any social friends the family had away from the business?"

"No, not at this time, but I'm hoping our interviews will lead us to some. To be sure, this family wasn't semi-hermits or anti-social."

When Timbo woke up Thursday morning, he was lying next to Adam on the big bed, not his cot. He tickled Adam's nose and laughed. Adam opened his eyes, grabbed hold of him, and tickled him silly.

"I don't know about you, but I have to use the bathroom, Timbo."

Timbo jumped off the bed, ran into the bathroom and closed the door. He laughed and said, "Ha, Ha, I beat you, Adam."

"Don't take all day, because I have to go bad, young man."

Shortly, Timbo opened the door before he washed his hands and face. Adam went in and thought, "I guess this is going to be a regular routine from now on."

"Do you shave yet, Adam?"

"Of course, I do smarty pants. I want to look good for the ladies, especially Mandy."

"I really like Ms. Mandy, and she's pretty like my mom."

"Mandy is a very special woman filled with lots of love."

"I think Aunt Mabel is very funny wearing those big hats and bunny rabbit slippers."

"Ms. Mabel is a special, funny woman, too. Now, let's put our robes and slippers on, and go down for breakfast."

When the fellers walked into the kitchen, Timbo ran around hugging everybody and kissed the women's cheeks. Mandy picked him up and gave him a big bear hug and kiss.

Mabel looked at Timbo and asked, "Well, good morning, young man. Are you hungry for a good breakfast?"

"I'm hungry enough to eat a pony, I think."

Everyone laughed and Adam said, "I'm hungry enough to eat an elephant."

Timbo looked at Adam and said, "An elephant is too big to eat, but you might be able to eat a pony."

Mabel replied, "I don't cook either one, so you'll have to be satisfied with eggs, bacon, grits, and toast, today."

Everyone gathered around the kitchen table while Timbo fed the dogs. Before he put the dog food away and sat at the table, Pixie and Dixie were right by his feet. He shook his finger at them and said, "I told you last night you eat too fast. Don't you listen?"

The dogs looked at each other and thought, "We eat fast all the time; it's you humans who eat, slowly. Don't worry; we're on the job with full tummies, little man."

Everyone laughed at the dog show, and Mabel blessed the meal. Obviously, Timbo loved eggs, grits, and toast. He asked for more grits, finished them off, and drank all his orange juice. Suddenly, he burped a loud one, crinkled his nose, and said, "Sorry folks that came out too fast."

Mabel giggled and said, "That's okay, because sometimes you can't help it. Take Aunt Millie here, she burps and passes gas out loud even though she doesn't mean to. She can't help that her body is a gas factory."

Millie looked shocked and said, "Mind your manners, sister dear."

Timbo asked, "Do you mean she farts a lot?"

Mabel replied, "She sure does."

Everybody laughed until their sides hurt, because Mabel just had to stir that bucket of poop. Timbo laughed and asked, "Aunt Millie, do you say excuse me?"

"Of course, I do young feller."

"That's good, because that's being polite, Aunt Millie. My mommy told me one time the older people got, the more they passed gas and the more it smelled. Is that true for you?"

Mandy answered, "Your mommy was right."

The ladies decided to clear the table and clean up before the fart session got out of hand. Leave it to Mabel for causing an uproar at breakfast.

Adam thought Millie was going to ring Mabel's neck like a chicken. Erika and Sheridan could never remember laughing this much in their whole lives. They couldn't wait to tell Dan, Dolly, Cody, and Art about this fart discussion.

Adam and Timbo went upstairs to get dressed, because they had to feed Millie's wild kingdom. Adam thought, "How is Timbo going to react to Mr. and Mrs. Greedy Gut? What is going to come out of that little boy's mouth next?"

The two went downstairs and loaded up with bird seed, suet, and peanuts. Adam said, "Thanks a lot for helping me feed the wild kingdom, because I need help filling feeders every day. Now, we are Aunt Millie's official wild kingdom caretakers."

Timbo remarked, "Aunt Millie must feed all the birds, squirrels, and chipmunks in Virginia."

The guys filled up all the feeders, suet cages, threw lots of peanuts around, and filled up the six birdbaths. Timbo looked at Adam and said, "This is a lot of fun feeding all these critters. What do we do with the plate full of peanut butter crackers?"

"The crackers are for a very special squirrel couple called Mr. and Mrs. Greedy Gut. Let's go inside, sit by the patio doors, and wait for them to come up to the doors. Mandy will show you how to feed them the crackers."

Mandy got Timbo and Adam all set up for the Greedy Gut Show. The little boy put the plate of crackers next to him on the floor to await the couple.

Adam had a notebook and pen next to him on the floor, so the two guys could write down all the birds and varmints they saw at Millie's wild kingdom buffet. Adam was surprised Timbo could identify so many birds.

All of a sudden, Timbo squealed, shook Adam's arm, and pointed at the fat ass squirrel couple waddling up to the patio doors.

Adam opened the sliding door slightly, and Timbo slipped

a cracker through the door. Mr. Greedy Gut grabbed the cracker and took off like greased lightning. The boy pushed another cracker through, and Mrs. Greedy Gut grabbed hers. Timbo jumped up and down, squealed, ran into the kitchen, and launched himself at Mandy laughing like a hyena!

He shouted, "They grabbed the crackers out of my hands, and I saw all kinds of different birds. Adam and I are keeping a list of everything we see!"

Mandy replied, "That's wonderful Timbo! Don't forget, Mr. and Mrs. Greedy Gut come back two more times."

Erika said, "Timbo, the couple is coming back."

He tore back to the sliding doors with Mandy and Mabel in tow, so he could show them how he fed them. Two more crackers went out the door, and the couple sprinted away like their fur was on fire. He ran around the room hugging everybody making sure they all saw what he did. The adults couldn't help but laugh at how excited he got feeding those crazy squirrels.

Sheridan added, "Get ready, Timbo, they're coming back for more."

Of course, the scene repeated itself, and Timbo went through his ritual, again. He begged Mandy to let him do the feeding every day. Mandy told him yes, because he needed to help Adam feed all the varmints every day, as well as Pixie and Dixie. The dogs couldn't understand why Timbo got so excited about two dumb, fat ass squirrels eating like pigs.

Mabel looked at Mandy and said, "I wish I had all that

energy he's got running through him, because he has enough to power this house for a year."

Mandy answered, "You are so right! I love how he gets so excited."

Timbo looked at Adam and asked, "Will the chipmunks come up here to get a peanut?"

"I don't know, but we sure don't want a chipmunk to get in the house, because we'd never find it."

Sheridan suggested, "Maybe, you can line up several peanuts leading to the door, so you can watch them up close."

"That would be a lot of fun, so I'm going to do that, tomorrow."

Cody walked into the family room just in time to see the last Greedy Gut feeding frenzy. Of course, he gave the boy a big hug and tickled him. Cody went over to Sheridan and kissed her forehead. They talked for a while, and she told him about the fart lesson at breakfast. He laughed until his sides hurt, then finally, went upstairs to put his suitcase in Adam's room. He made one more guard in the house to keep Timbo safe and watch over Sheridan.

Cobra ate lunch thinking about the next step to the plan. Now, was not the time to panic; just stay calm and in control. The police presence was just a bump in the road at this point. The plan was like a chess game to Cobra, and Cobra knew how to move the pieces. No one knows which pieces will be moved to complete the plan. *"Some pieces think they are important, but won't they be surprised when they are no longer needed. I use people as long as they are needed, then they become trash to get rid of. Trust no one when it comes to murder. Watch your back, because there is always someone who wants to put a dagger in it. Only one person can have the ultimate prize, and that person is me."*

CHAPTER 5

Mandy and Adam went line dancing Thursday night, because they enjoyed the exercise and being with each other.

Before calling it a night, Adam looked into Mandy's eyes and said, "I want you to know I think you are very pretty with a gentle heart and soul. You have such a caring spirit with boundless love ready to share with the people around you. I love you very much, Mandy. You've changed my life forever, and I want you to marry me.

Mandy jumped into his arms and kissed him silly. "Adam, I love you very much, too, and the answer is yes!"

He said, "I knew I loved you when we went to Art and Dolly's wedding, and I didn't like the other guys dancing with you."

Mandy laughed and said, "I noticed you weren't a happy camper."

"There's something else, Mandy. That precious little boy is part of our destiny. I already love him. How do you feel about him?"

"When he ran into my arms and sobbed, I felt like he was my son. I felt like I was to love and keep him safe."

"Sweetheart, I feel the same way!"

"Adam, I don't want a big wedding like Dolly's. I'd like to get married at the farmhouse surrounded by our close friends."

"I'd like that, too. Just think, when the stone farmhouse is ready it will be our new home. Both of us will help Millie and Mabel like we always do."

"That's right!"

"Let's get married before Christmas."

Mandy thought a bit then said, "Shiloh and Darren's wedding is December 12th. How about December 19th, because Mabel is flying to Wisconsin on the sixth to visit her daughter's family and flying back on the eleventh, so she doesn't miss Shiloh's wedding?"

"That's fantastic! This weekend we'll go shopping for your engagement ring and have dinner at an expensive restaurant. I'll ask Millie if I can start moving my things into the stone farmhouse, so I can vacate my apartment."

"This is wonderful, Adam. We can start setting up our new home by getting the things it needs."

Adam and Mandy headed back to the farmhouse very much in love and happy. They both knew they wanted to adopt Timmy and keep him safe. Destiny brought their three lives together for a reason, and Becky was right in the middle of it. They decided to tell everyone the good news when Art and Dolly came over Friday to bring several things from Timmy's room.

Friday morning, Task Force Bronner arrived at the

pharmaceutical company to start their interviews with the employees. Detective Gage sat down in Dr. Lim's office and started asking questions.

"Before we continue the interview, I want to show you this document signed by Dr. Bronner, my lawyer, and myself. You will see that Dr. Bronner gave me part ownership of the company to get me to leave Richfield Pharmaceuticals. I didn't feel comfortable coming here when there were others already here who were just as well qualified as I was. He insisted I come, because we were such close friends going back to our college days."

Gage remarked, "So, Dr. Bronner gave you twenty-five percent of the business with an option to buy a larger part of the company?"

"That is correct."

Gage asked, "Where were you between 3:30 pm and 4:30 pm the day Dr. Bronner and his family were murdered?"

"I was meeting with Vernell Cleveland concerning the company's government contracts, because I wanted to know exactly what medicines we were sending to the military hospitals and clinics. Vernell went over all the printouts with me to make sure I didn't miss anything."

Gage asked, "How long did this meeting take?"

"We met from 2:30 pm to 5:00 pm before we decided to stop for the day and resume the next morning."

"Did you know Dr. Bronner's wife was pregnant?"

"Oh yes, Kurt was so excited and quite proud to be a father at age forty-five."

"Can you think of anyone who would want to kill them?"

"I can't imagine anyone wanting to kill them, because they were wonderful people. I'm still in shock and have no idea what I should do next."

Gage answered, "Continue to operate as usual until law enforcement has a chance to go through the will and other documents. The court will decide what to do in this case after all the facts are in."

Hansen's interview with Dr. Maxine Stine was a real eye opener. According to her, Dr. Bronner was a brilliant, kind man, but his judge of character was poor.

She said Dr. Newby was a real bastard who stomped on a lot of people to get to the top. He stole other colleague's ideas and claimed they were his. When this was brought to Dr. Bronner's attention, he refused to do anything about it saying he was not going to get involved in employee cat fights.

Dr. Stine stated she was very upset when Dr. Bronner went outside the company and hired Dr. Lim, because she felt several could have been promoted to deputy CEO already in the company. When asked where she was at the time of the murder, she said she was working until 5:00 pm.

Agent Ryan Creekmore's interview produced a wealth of clues. Dr. Elwood Harris stated Dr. Newby was a gold digging bastard who had no business being deputy CEO.

Newby stole other scientist's ideas, and convinced Dr. Bronner they were his. Dr. Harris said Dr. Bronner never got down in the trenches with his scientists to see what was really going on. Also, he was mad that the new deputy CEO came from the West Coast. In his opinion, someone should have been promoted within the company. Elwood stated he was at work until 5:00 pm the day of the murder.

When Ryan talked with Maria Santana, she stated she disliked Newby and was glad he was dead. According to her, Newby only cared about himself and was never a team player. When asked about Dr. Bronner, she broke into tears saying he was such a wonderful family man and boss. She couldn't believe anyone would want to murder the family. Santana stated she was home with a sinus infection when the murder occurred.

Agent Byron Sawyer interviewed Dr. Bronner's secretary Hansa Fareed. The poor woman sobbed almost the whole time. Byron did find out Greta Bronner played the piano, because she played at the company's Christmas party. Also, she told Sawyer Dr. Bronner suffered from migraine headaches and went home early, often. When he had a bad one, he had to lie down after he took his medicine. When asked where she was the day of the murder, she stated she went home with female issues around 2:00 pm. Fareed said she disliked Newby, Stine, and Zocrist, because they were snobs.

Agent Brad Donahue's interview with Dillon Carr added more clues. He was aware of Dr. Newby's tricks, but stayed away from the scientists. In his opinion, all those white coats were a bit conceded and strange. He stated he could understand why Dr. Bronner hired a new deputy CEO from outside the company, because there was too much jealousy among the possible candidates. When asked about his opinion of Dr. Bronner, he added the man was brilliant, but had no idea how to deal with employees who were at each other's throats.

When told the police had requested an audit be done concerning the company's finances, Carr stated he would help in any way possible. When asked where he was the day of the murder, he answered he was home sick with the flu.

Art and Dolly arrived at Millie's farmhouse before lunch and carried in several boxes from Timmy's room. When the little boy saw them, he ran up to them and hugged them both. Art picked him up and gave him a big bear hug, and Dolly hugged and kissed him silly. Of course, Timbo had to tell them about the birds and Mr. and Mrs. Greedy Gut.

Somehow, Mabel steered the conversation back to breakfast and the fart session. Art and Dolly laughed until their sides hurt knowing Mabel dodged a serious pillow fight with Millie over that stinky bucket of poop.

Timbo looked at Art and asked, "I don't like calling you Mr. Art. Can I call you Pop-Pop?"

"Of course, you can, little man."

Timbo looked at Dolly and asked, "Can I call you Nana?"

"Sure you can."

"That's good, because Becky said you're going to be my new grandparents."

Dolly answered, "Becky is right; you'll be our new grandson, and we'll help keep you safe."

Art put Timbo in his lap when he sat down, so he could tell him about the tutor he hired to home school him for the time being.

Dolly took the 3M ladies in the kitchen to talk, privately. She let Millie know the two had joint custody of Timbo, and gave her the papers from Judge Franklin.

Dolly looked at Mabel and Millie and asked, "I've never been a mother, so how do I go about telling the boy about the boxes from his room?"

Millie answered, "Tell him he can't go back to his home, because it's not safe. Let him know the police put a lot of his things from his room in boxes, so you could bring them over."

Dolly continued, "Judge Franklin has given me permission to take anything from the house, that isn't evidence, to save for Timbo."

Mabel asked, "What things are you referring to?"

"Things like pictures, photo albums, jewelry, his bed, and anything else he might want or cherish."

Mandy remarked, "We could ask him to make a list of things he wants."

Dolly added, "That's a good idea. Detective Gage, Vince, Kris, David, Robert, and Lydia are going over to the Bronner home on Sunday, so Art and I can get things out of the house."

Mandy spoke up and said, "Maybe, you can store things at the stone farmhouse for him."

"That's a great idea, Mandy. If the Bronner house is put up for sale, it will have to be cleaned out, plus the crime scene needs to be cleaned."

Millie added, "Dolly, don't forget the attic, garage, and a shed."

"Lord, that's right! There might be Christmas ornaments and lights in the attic along with family keepsakes."

Mabel remarked, "The stone farmhouse is ready to move into, but there's very little furniture in it. Mrs. Lancaster's furniture was in bad shape, and even her towels were thread bare."

Dolly asked Millie, "Can we move a lot of things into the stone farmhouse?"

"Bring over whatever you want, because everything belongs to Timbo, now."

After the group ate lunch, Timbo was told about the house and the boxes from his room. Even though he was very sad, he was glad to go through the boxes containing his things. He and Mandy made a list of things he wanted from his home and then he dropped a bombshell when he told them his daddy had a safe in the wall in his room behind the Star Wars poster. He told them the combination, so they could empty it out.

Before Art and Dolly left, Adam called everybody together and told them he'd asked Mandy to marry him. The couple let everyone know they were getting married on December 19th at Millie's farmhouse. There were tons of hugs and kisses exchanged along with some tears of joy.

Timbo was caught up in the celebration, because he knew he belonged with Adam and Mandy, somehow. Adam got Art off to the side and told him they wanted to adopt Timbo.

Art looked at Adam and said, "I'll get the wheels turning to make it happen, because I can see the bond that has formed between the three of you."

Mabel spoke up and said, "I love planning weddings, so you two don't worry about a thing. Millie and I will throw you a fantastic wedding and reception fit for the Queen of England."

Millie added, "We'll have the place all decorated for Christmas with a beautiful tree right here in the family room you can get married next to."

Adam said, "You ladies are the best. I want you to know how much I appreciate everything you have done for me and how much you have changed my life."

He went over and hugged Millie and Mabel with tears in

his eyes. He looked at Dolly and said, "I won't let you down, because Mandy and I will help the ladies run the safe house network from now on."

Dolly replied, "I know you will." Art and Dolly said their goodbyes and headed back home, because Ernesto and Rosarita were moving into the cottage behind Art's garage, tomorrow. The couple loved their new home, and they were eager to get moved in.

Ernesto was Dolly's driver/bodyguard for security reasons, because Dolly couldn't drive by herself. Rosarita was hired as housekeeper and chef to help Dolly take care of their new home.

Late Saturday afternoon, Art and Dolly went to his son's birthday party in Leesburg. Art already had Ken's present parked in his sister's garage.

When his son saw the 1965 burgundy and white Chevy El Camino classic car fully restored and ready to drive, he almost went crazy. Ken hugged his dad and Dolly for giving him such a wonderful gift.

Art's grandchildren had to bring Dolly up to date concerning their social lives, and all of them were excited about spending Thanksgiving with them.

On Sunday, Detective Gage met Art, Dolly, and her helpers at the Bronner home. Robert rented a medium size U-Haul truck with lots of boxes in it.

The first thing Gage did was open the wall safe in Timmy's room.

"Holy smokes; this safe is full, so let's see what we have here." He pulled out everything and put it on the bed. "Here are birth certificates, U. S. passports, a marriage license, titles to the cars, title to the house, and title to land and a cabin in Rappahannock County near Smedley, Virginia on the Covington River. Here are life insurance policies on Dr. Bronner and Mrs. Bronner for $500,000 each, and life insurance policies on Greta and Timothy for $250,000 each. Here's $8,000 in cash, and look at all this jewelry. This is not costume stuff; this is the real deal."

Dolly said, "Timmy said the jewelry belonged to his mother and grandmother."

Gage stated, "A lot of this stuff needs to be in a safe deposit box, and these life insurance policies need to be taken care of. Since we have the car titles and the titles to the homes, those can be sold, and the money be put into a trust for the boy."

Art replied, "Dolly and I will meet with Judge Franklin and find out what he wants us to do about all this. We have to make sure everything is legal and protects everything for the boy."

Gage asked, "Do you have a safe at home or at Freestone, Dolly?"

"I have both."

"Then, take these things to Freestone and put them in the

safe for right now."

The group looked at Timmy's list and started moving those things into David and Robert's trucks. Next, they moved all the bedroom furniture, towels, sheets, blankets, and bedspreads. Next, they moved everything in the kitchen including the food which went into Art's Suburban. Lastly, they took the best pictures off the walls, packed up photo albums, photos around the house, and emptied out the freezer which went into Vince's Explorer.

The group decided to come back next weekend and move some more things. They headed to the stone farmhouse to unload the U-Haul truck and put as much as they could away until next weekend. When that was finished, they headed to Millie's farmhouse to unload the rest.

Art thought it was a good idea to take Timmy's toy chest in first, so he would be occupied while they unloaded the rest. Vince and David took the chest and headed for the family room. The guys put it down just as Timmy came down the hall. He saw his beloved toy chest and ran over to it as tears ran down his face. Vince picked him up, held him close, and comforted the boy while he cried. Kris came up to him and patted his back telling him he was safe and very much loved.

Finally, Timbo looked at Vince and said, "Thank you for getting my toy chest, Mr. Vince. Becky told me you were her cousin, and you look like her daddy."

"That's right, young man."

Timbo looked at Kris and said, "You are very pretty, and you can see Becky just like Mr. Vince."

"Oh yes, Timmy, I've seen and talked to her."

The little tike pointed his finger and said, "You are David, and you got hurt in a war."

"That's right, little feller. We brought you everything on your list, so we better bring in the rest for you."

"I'm going to learn sign language, so I can talk to you better."

David signed thank you, and the boy clapped his hands and giggled."

Timbo took Adam by the hand and led him over to the toy chest, so he could show Adam what treasures he kept inside. Millie let Vince know there was room to put Timmy's bed in Adam's room, so she went upstairs to remove the cot. Art and Robert brought the food inside, so the ladies could put it away. Detective Gage helped Vince and David bring in the bed, bike, skateboard, camera, and all the other things he asked for.

Vince looked at Kris and said, "He is a precious boy, Sugar. I hope we will be blessed with a son like him."

"I hope so, too."

Gage said, "Timbo sure likes Adam. Look at the two of them going through that chest."

Dolly walked into the family room and laughed at the treasure hunt.

Gage asked, "Dolly, since you are a lawyer, can I ask Timbo some questions, or do you think that's not a good idea, right now?"

"You can ask him some questions; just try not to upset him. The boy has a genius IQ, so he should be easy to talk to."

The two walked over to Adam and Timbo, so Dolly could introduce Detective Gage. Adam sat down with Timbo in his lap, and Gage shook both of their hands.

Gage said, "I'm going to find the bad person who took your family's lives. It's very important that no one knows you're here, but the people in this house."

Timbo said, "You don't want the bad person to find me."

"That's right. Did you see the bad person break into your house?"

"No, I was running through the woods with Becky to get to Aunt Millie's, so I could get help for my mommy, daddy, and sissy."

"How did you know they needed help?"

"Becky told me."

Now, Detective Gage didn't believe in ghosts and all that supernatural bull, but he decided to keep an open mind.

"Do you know why you can't go home or back to Stargate

Academy?"

"Yes, because it's not safe for me."

"Do you know of anyone who wanted to hurt your family?"

"No, sir."

"Was your mommy and daddy happy about the baby?"

"Oh yes, they did a lot of hugging, kissing, and patting mommy's tummy."

"Did your mommy and daddy have friends who came over to your house to visit?"

"We did a lot of things with Mr. and Mrs. Madison. We'd have cookouts together, we went camping, and we went to Busch Gardens this summer with them."

"Do you remember their first names?"

"John and Wendy."

"Did the Madison's have children?"

"Sure, Heidi was one of Greta's best friends at school and church, and I like to play with Hunter."

"Do you know their address and phone number?"

Gage wrote down what Timbo told him, and the name of the church and minister. "Did your parents have any other close friends?"

"We went to the beach with Mr. and Mrs. Vogel,

sometimes. I could play with Aidan, and we were in the same Sunday school class."

"Do you remember their first names?"

"Jim and Penny, but I don't know their address or phone number."

"That's okay, we'll find it. Do you know Dr. Michael Lim?"

"Oh yes, he's been best friends with my daddy, forever. I like him a lot, because he's funny and real nice. Usually, he visits us over once a year."

"Did you have babysitters, sometimes?"

"Mrs. Parrish and Hanny were the only babysitters we had."

"Who's Hanny?"

"She's daddy's secretary at work."

"Did you like these ladies?"

"Oh yes, they were a lot of fun."

"Timmy thanks a lot for talking to me. The police are doing everything we can to catch this bad person. Is there anything else you want to tell me?"

"I really love it here, and I know they will keep me safe."

"That's good to hear."

The entire group visited and enjoyed a delicious meal

prepared by Mabel and Mandy.

Dolly noticed Timbo interacted with everyone like he'd known them all along, and she felt the bond he had with Adam and Mandy. Somehow, she knew they would make wonderful parents and would guide Timbo through life's ups and downs. Dolly thought, "I might not have been a mother, but I intend to be a wonderful grandmother to Art's grandchildren and little Timbo."

After the meal was finished and the kitchen was cleaned up, the group said their goodbyes and headed home.

Dolly, Art, and Detective Gage stopped by Freestone to put the Bronner family valuables and papers in the safe.

Dolly and Art had an appointment with Judge Franklin and the Bronner family's minister on Monday. Detective Gage and the task force would head back to Bronner Pharmaceuticals on Monday to continue their employee interviews which he expected to run over into Tuesday.

Wednesday, he wanted to sit down with the task force and start going over all the interviews. The task force would enjoy Thanksgiving with their families and meet on Friday to continue their investigation.

CHAPTER 6

On Monday, Task Force Bronner was back at the company interviewing more employees. Detective Gage couldn't talk with Dr. Colin Zocrist until today, because Zocrist had a dentist appointment. Their talk was very similar to those of the other major players. He disliked Dr. Newby and called him a smooth talking liar who should have never been promoted to deputy CEO. He felt Dr. Bronner should have promoted someone in the company, not go all the way to the West Coast to hire a new deputy. Zocrist thought Dr. Bronner was a kind, brilliant man, but not a people person.

Brad's interview with the head of shipping and receiving yielded another flu victim who just returned on Monday. The man said he liked Dr. Bronner, but the rest of the white coats he wasn't crazy about, because they were arrogant and strange. When asked to define strange, he said they acted like they were on a different planet.

He said, "I know these people have lots of brains, but I'm not a stupid shit. At least, treat me with respect like I do them. Crap man, they go to the bathroom just like me!"

Byron was quite intrigued with his interview with Dr. Clara Beach, the senior scientist in the Research Division. She disliked both Dr. Newby and Dr. Stine, because she thought both of them were gold diggers who believed they walked on water. The woman liked Dr. Bronner's decision to hire someone outside the company to replace Newby. In her opinion, there was way too much jealousy going on among the top scientists. She said the head of security thought he was a super stud who could take care of all the ladies at the company. She stated she was working until 4:30 pm the day the family was killed.

Byron thought, "Lord, this company was like jumping into shark infested waters covered in blood."

Hansen's interview with Vernell Cleveland confirmed her meeting with Dr. Lim, and she provided some interesting details that would need further investigation. According to her, Dr. Zocrist and Maria Santana had the hots for one another. She happened to see the good doctor running his hands all over Maria's behind during a passionate kiss. What the good doctor didn't know was Harry Dent, Dillon Carr, Jesse Rice, and Dr. Tanner were all doing the same thing to Maria.

Supposedly, Dr. Maxine Stine divorced her husband after she caught him running around with one of the girls in the IT Department. Vernell said she fired the girl before Dr. Stine went to Dr. Bronner about the situation.

Vernell said, "I don't know why I get caught up in these messes. I don't care who runs around with whom. This company is a regular hotbed of gossip. Lord, detective, I go home some nights with my head spinning from all the tales I hear or bad behavior I see."

Agent Creekmore visited Stargate Academy on Monday. The founder and principal of the academy greeted the agent with much sadness in her heart. She was shocked and angry someone would murder three from that wonderful family. She was beside herself knowing Timmy was missing. She went on to describe Timmy as brilliant, delightful, well behaved, funny, and eager to learn. He was one of three child prodigies her school was teaching. Timmy's father and mother were wonderful parents who were very active in his curriculum choices, and they made it clear they wanted their son to enjoy his childhood with children around his age. They didn't want him to be a five year old adult.

Timmy was not enrolled year round, because his parents wanted him to enjoy his summers just being a kid. The owner stated she wished a lot of her other parents felt the same way. When asked about the piano, she smiled and said, "His piano teacher could listen to him play for hours. The teacher said it wouldn't be long before Timmy would pass her and need someone more professional as in a college professor to teach him."

When asked about the parent's social life, the woman didn't know anything about that, but she said, "Timmy used to talk a lot about a boy he played and went to the beach with, and I think the boy's name was Aidan."

Creekmore asked, "Was he a neighbor, or did he go to school with his sister, Greta?"

"I'm sorry, I have no idea."

The agent asked, "Did you know Mrs. Bronner was pregnant?"

"Timmy was so excited about the baby being a boy, so he could have a playmate. That monster murdered four people in the family, not three. Please, find Timmy!"

"We will find him."

"Please let me know when the funeral takes place. One last thing, I want to show you Timmy's desk and work area."

When they got there, the area was filled with cards, stuffed animals, written notes, and flowers. The woman wiped tears from her eyes while Ryan took several deep breaths. He pulled out his camera and took a picture for future use.

Agent Brad Donahue went to Greta's school to meet with the guidance counselor and principal. The whole administration and student body were shocked and outraged over this senseless murder. Greta was a popular student who played on the soccer and volleyball teams and was a straight A student. Her parents and brother came to her games, and her parents always came to all the parent-teacher meetings. When asked about Greta playing the piano, they were proud to say the girl was the best musical student the school ever had.

The principal showed Brad a bulletin board in the school lobby that was a memorial to Greta. There were notes written to her, cards, stuffed animals, and flowers. Brad couldn't help but swallow a knot in his throat, so he pulled his camera out and took a picture. He promised to let the school know about the funeral arrangements as soon as he knew.

The school didn't know about any social friendships the family had, but the principal let Brad talk to Greta's best friends.

One girl told him their parents had rented a house on the beach together, so everyone could enjoy a week of swimming and fun. The girl remembered the house was in Nags Head, North Carolina. Brad went on and found out the parents went out to dinner, had cookouts, went to church, and the kids enjoyed sleepovers together. This friendship seemed to match what Detective Gage found out from the boy.

Byron interviewed Dr. Rose Smith, the senior scientist in the Testing Division. She stated Dr. Harris was easy to work with and was quite capable of being the deputy CEO. She couldn't understand why he wasn't chosen when Dr. Newby was killed. However, if Dr. Bronner wanted someone from outside the company, she figured he knew what he was doing. When asked about Dr. Newby, she said he was a first class prick who tried to get into her drawers.

She said, "I wouldn't go to bed with him if he was the last man on earth. His poor wife didn't seem to know he was prowling around for some fresh boobs. Excuse me for being so blunt, Agent Sawyer."

Byron asked, "Did Dr. Newby put the make on other women in the company?"

"Agent, there were lots of rumors going around, but I have no idea if they were true or just gossip."

"We can follow the rumors and see if they're true or not."

"Okay, I heard he put the make on Dr. Stine's secretary, a female security guard, Hansa Fareed, Maria Santana, and a woman in the IT Department. I guess he thought he was so handsome all the women would jump his bones."

When asked about Dr. Bronner, she broke into tears saying he and his family were wonderful people who didn't hurt anyone. She stated she was at work until 3:30 pm the day of the murder.

Dolly and Art met with Judge Franklin and told him what was found in the wall safe and what they knew, so far. She showed the judge the insurance papers and the will. Since Dolly was appointed Timmy's legal guardian and trustee of his estate, the judge gave her instructions on how to deal with the following issues: the will, life insurance policies, bills concerning the house, sale of any property, funeral arrangements, and moving the wall safe contents from Freestone to a safe deposit box. The judge gave Dolly signed legal documents she would need to handle the boy's estate. This little boy was going to have a very large trust fund when he became an adult.

When they left Judge Franklin, Art and Dolly had lunch, went to the post office to have the Bronner mail sent to her, and then went to the bank where the Bronner accounts were to get things changed over, so she could manage the estate and pay bills. They got a safe deposit box, so she could move Timmy's things out of Freestone's safe.

Next, they met with the minister at the Bronner's church. It was quite apparent the congregation was shocked and grieving. As they talked to the minister, they learned the Bronner's were private people who stood in the shadows to perform their Christian deeds. For example, the church's food bank, soup kitchen, and clothes closet were funded by Dr. Bronner. Also, he donated money to any church member who fell on hard times, because they lost their job or had large medical bills. Also, he bought the church a van, so they could deliver meals to their elderly members who were unable to cook and shop for groceries.

Dolly asked how much money it took to fund the bank, kitchen, and closet for a month. When the minister told her, she took out her checkbook and wrote out a check to cover the next six months.

The minister was shocked, but very thankful for her generous donation.

She informed him there would be a check sent to the church every six months to honor Dr. Bronner's generosity and memory. She asked if the clothes closet could use the Bronner clothing, and the minister said they would love to have the clothes.

The three agreed the memorial service would be held at the church on Monday evening at 7:00 pm, and the burial would be private due to the situation.

Dolly thought she was going back to work Tuesday, but that went out the window with recent events. Thank heavens; Vince agreed to hang on as acting director until November 30th. Freestone would be closed Thanksgiving and the day after, but the task force and some others would be in and out on that Friday.

Dolly and Art went to the grocery store to stock up for Thanksgiving and dropped by the florist to pick up flower arrangements she ordered earlier. When they got home, Ernesto and Rosarita helped bring everything in.

Tuesday, all four were going to decorate the house for Thanksgiving and throw in Christmas, too. Dolly always put her Christmas tree up before Thanksgiving, because she loved looking at it. Since she put that much work into it, she planned to enjoy her handiwork. Art loved the idea and couldn't wait to see Dolly transform their home into a Christmas palace. His family was going to be shocked when they walked into their Dad's new home on Thanksgiving Day.

Ernesto and Rosarita really liked Dolly, because she was the best thing that happened to Mr. Art. They were so glad to be back with Mr. Art, and Ernesto knew Mr. Art really loved Dolly with all his heart. Those two were meant for each other, because she changed his life and brought him out of his seclusion.

Monday was business as usual at Freestone. Vince got comfortable at his desk, because he had to go over his investigative team assignments. Homeland Security wanted

Freestone to handle another case. He had an appointment at 1:00 pm with a family who wanted Freestone to look into a cold case from Prince William County.

Team 1 and 2 were still working their Justice Department cases. Team 3 was working their missing person's case. Team 4 was on down time after Task Force Curtain, but Cody McCaslin was on the security detail at Millie's. When Travis Spangler got back from down time, he might assign him to Task Force Bronner. Team 5 was still working their murder cold case. Team 6 was on down time after Task Force Curtain, and when they got back he would assign them the Homeland Security case. Team 7 was working Task Force Bronner. Team 8 was working their Justice Department case, but they were very close to solving it. All they needed was one day to confirm their findings. Team 9 and 10 were still working their missing person's cold cases.

Vince wasn't sure how he was going to handle another case, right now. After he talked with this family, he would have to make a decision on whether to take the case or not. If things kept going the way they were, he might have to form a new investigative team.

Vince let his mind wander to the holidays, because he was anxious to see how Kris was going to decorate their home. They were spending Thanksgiving with his in-laws, David, Heather, and Heather's parents who were driving up from Ashville, North Carolina.

David planned to give Heather her engagement ring while her parents were here. They decided to get married in August, but they hadn't picked the date, yet.

Kris told him Friday and Saturday they were decorating their home for Christmas. She had bought Christmas decorations, lights, and ornaments to decorate, so he knew it was just about show time. They were going out for dinner Wednesday evening after work and then buy a Christmas tree. Kris loved the Christmas holidays, so Vince knew his wife was going all out to make their home a Christmas wonderland.

Vince thought with a smile, "Well, Peaches, this is your first Christmas; I wonder what kind of a mess you're going to make? Kris will spank your behind if you get into the tree."

When the phone rang, Vince snapped back to the present and answered it. Homeland Security was sending Freestone packets on their case, they discussed some details, and they agreed Team 6 could start the case November 30th.

Vince knew Nathan Donovan, Vickie Donovan Tierney, and Mr. and Mrs. Donovan were going to stop by Freestone after a medal ceremony at Fort Belvoir Army Base.

Nathan was an army medic who served in Afghanistan where he was wounded dragging several wounded comrades under heavy fire to safety.

Vince wanted to shake his hand for his service and bravery under fire. Men like Nathan and Eric Tierney put their lives on the line to protect our freedom, but some like Captain Bryan Amherst (his wife's first husband) didn't come home alive, because he gave his life, so we could enjoy that freedom.

Sierra buzzed the Donovan family into Freestone, and she just about passed out stone, cold dead when she saw a man wearing Army dress blues with medals all over his chest. She welcomed them to Freestone and called Vince to let him know the family was here.

Vince came out of his office and proceeded to hug and kiss the ladies and shake the men's hands. It was almost like a family reunion, because the Donovan's were very close to Kris, David, and Vince. Vince went around the work stations introducing them, and then they headed back to his office, so they could visit.

Shontelle said, "Sierra, put your eyeballs back in your head, and your tongue back in your mouth. Do you know how stupid you look? I can drive a motorhome through your mouth."

Sierra remarked, "Isn't he one drop dead, handsome man?"

Shontelle answered, "It's that dress blue uniform that's sent you over the crazy cliff."

"He takes my breath away and makes my head feel funny."

Diana chimed in, "Honey, your head feels funny all the time."

Jason chimed in and said, "Sierra, take several deep breaths before you pass out on us."

"Oh my, he could be my Prince Charming anytime."

Shontelle said, "He's probably a Prince Charming butthole."

Jason fired back, "He doesn't look like Prince Charming to me."

"That's because you are a man, bonehead."

"Well, thanks for noticing that, Sierra."

Diana piped in, "Good Lord, you're going to walk around for the rest of the day with stars in your eyes and your head in a cloud."

"He is so handsome."

Diana fired back, "He looks like road kill."

Jason chimed in, "You're right, Diana. Plus, she's going to be a useless, twit brain for the rest of the day."

"He probably thinks I'm an ugly toad."

Shontelle added, "When he comes out, I'll ask him that."

"Don't you dare, Shontelle! If he thought I looked like an ugly toad, I'd be devastated."

Jason fired back, "No, he would think you're a silly toad."

"You are such a smart butt, Jason."

Diana said, "Lord, I think you are having a hot flash like Mabel."

"I'm not having a hot flash; it's just hot in here."

Shontelle shot back, "I can see smoke coming out of your

ears, girl."

Jason added, "It's your britches that's having a hot flash."

Diana chimed in, "You better be careful, or your britches well catch on fire."

Shontelle chimed in, "He rode up to Freestone on his magnificent white horse which is taking a dump on our sidewalk, right now."

"I'd ride on that white horse with him."

Jason shot back, "Sierra, you'd fall off the back of the horse and kill yourself."

Diana shot back, "You'd leave us to clean up its crap on the sidewalk? There is no way you're riding off in the sunset while we stand on the crappy sidewalk with our buckets and shovels."

Shontelle shouted, "Amen, brothers and sisters!"

The whole work station broke out in waves of laughter, and Sierra threw up her arms in surrender. She thought, "These people can scramble up anybody's brains, but she loved them no matter what."

With pride in her voice, Mrs. Donovan told Vince that Nathan was awarded the Silver Star and Purple Heart for his bravery under hostile fire saving the lives of five comrades.

Vince asked, "Were you badly wounded, Nathan?"

"No, I received a few shrapnel wounds which have healed up, nicely. Vince, I tell you that ambush came out of nowhere. We suffered four killed and eleven wounded in an area that was supposed to be secure and friendly. Over there you don't know whose an ally and who the Taliban is."

Vince asked, "Is your enlistment about up?"

"Come Wednesday, I'll be a civilian, and I start my new job December 14th at the hospital as an emergency room nurse."

Vince asked, "Where are you staying?"

"I'm staying in mom and dad's apartment over the garage until I save enough money to get a place of my own. I'm going out tomorrow evening to look for a car or a truck with the money I sent home while I was in Afghanistan."

Vince added, "Kris and I are looking forward to dinner, because I know your mom and sister will put on a feast, tonight. Before we go to lunch at the Deli, I want Julie from the photo lab to take some pictures of us with some of the Freestone employees."

When the group left Vince's office, Julie met them at the work station area. Jason was so glad to see Nathan, because they were friends in high school. He had a picture taken with Nathan and the family followed by Shontelle, Diana, Desiree, Heather, and Chad.

Shontelle asked, "Nathan, do you think our receptionist looks like a toad?"

Sierra wanted to crawl under her desk and cry, but Nathan walked over to her and took a good look.

He answered, "In my opinion, if she looks like a toad it's a mighty cute toad. I would like a picture taken with you, Sierra."

Julie snapped the picture, and Sierra just knew her face was fire engine red from embarrassment. He was so handsome, and she was Miss Plain Jane like an old shoe.

Nathan asked, "Sweetheart, would you write down your phone number for me? You can expect a call from me this weekend. My family has me all tied up until then?"

Sierra fumbled for her note pad, wrote her number down, and gave it to him. "Saturday, I'll be at Millie's farmhouse to help them decorate for Christmas."

He put the note in his wallet and gave Sierra a lights out smile. She felt like melting butter over popcorn. He told everyone goodbye as the group headed for the Deli to have lunch. When the door closed behind them, Sierra dropped in her chair, took several deep breaths, and tried to stop her legs from shaking.

Shontelle teased, "Lord, you're shaking like an earthquake; you better get control of yourself before the building falls down around us."

Diana asked, "Did you pee in your pants, toad?"

"No!"

Shontelle added, "I think you did, girl."

"He won't call me, because he was just being nice after you blabbed your mouth."

Jason asked, "What happened to your self-confidence?

What happened to that woman who busted her father's nose wide open? Trust me; he'll call you, honey."

"Do you really think so?"

Jason answered, "We've been friends a long time, so don't worry he'll call you."

Diana chimed in, "I hope you don't do something stupid like never washing your dress again, because he touched it."

"I'm not that stupid. I'm just a Plain Jane with no class, so he'll just call and that will be the end of it."

Shontelle got up out of her desk, stomped over to Sierra, shook her finger and said, "Sierra, so you think you're an old toad, a Plain Jane, and an old shoe. Well honey, you look worse than that, because you look like gorilla road kill."

Sierra looked at Shontelle and burst out laughing until tears ran down her cheeks. By then, the whole office was roaring with laughter. Finally, the group settled down and got back to work. Leave it to Shontelle to change the group into a kindergarten class on a sugar high in a skinny, southern belle minute.

When Vince got back from lunch, he looked at Sierra and said, "He will call you this weekend, so go ahead and have another hot flash or whatever you were having."

Diana added, "She had a hot flash and peed in her pants."

"I did not mess my pants! Thanks a lot for telling me that, Vince."

Vince stopped and said, "He said to tell you he thinks

you're cute as a kitten."

Jason piped in, "Dang, Nathan must need glasses, because Sierra isn't all furry."

Shontelle shot back, "Jason, when I look at your wife, I think she must have been blind to marry you. Honey, you look like monkey road kill."

Diana shouted, "Amen, brothers and sisters!"

Vince looked at Jason and said, "I guess the ladies just paid you a compliment, because monkey road kill is better than skunk road kill."

Diana said, "Sierra, make sure you clean the crap off the sidewalk left by his white horse."

"I'll get right on it, smarty pants. Amen, brothers and sisters!"

Vince left the group laughing as he went back into his office. When he sat down, a picture flashed in his mind of a pistol sitting in a desk drawer. Again, Vince was frustrated, because he could only guess that the weapon was a .38, but he wasn't sure. What did it mean? Did it have something to do with Dr. Bronner? He was starting to realize this was a progression of clues, so he wrote down exactly what he saw and when.

Vince met with the couple at 1:00 pm concerning their daughter's disappearance. The mother said, "Her husband wants people to think he is wonderful and devastated, but I believe in my heart he killed her and got rid of her body. He's the outdoors type who hunts, goes fishing, camps out, and hikes. He got rid of my daughter's body somewhere in the area he prowls around in. My girl disappeared in January of 2009, and two months later he was shacking up with some bimbo!"

Vince explained that Freestone couldn't start the case until December 3rd or the 4th, because that's when he'd have a team available to take the case.

The couple said they could wait, because they really wanted Freestone to work the case. Vince told them he would contact them when the team got started.

He walked the couple to the front and shook their hands. Vince hated what people went through when a loved one was missing. He knew he had to move some people around to make sure Freestone could work the case, because he didn't want to turn them away.

CHAPTER 7

On Tuesday, Task Force Bronner was back at Bronner Pharmaceuticals to continue their interviews.

Byron met with Dr. Roy Tanner, the senior scientist in the Production Division and was intrigued by their talk. He couldn't stand Dr. Newby, Dr. Zocrist, or Dr. Stine, because all three were gold diggers. He stated Dr. Stine was crazy in love with Newby, but he wasn't the least bit interested in her. Also, he agreed Dr. Bronner did the right thing in bringing Dr. Lim from the West Coast to be the next deputy CEO.

The man added another bit of gossip by saying, "He wouldn't be surprised if Newby, Zocrist, or Harry Dent was the father of the baby the woman in the IT Department is carrying. She claims her live in boyfriend is the father, but I don't buy that for a minute."

Brad's interview with Harry Dent left Brad's ears ringing. He was an arrogant prick who knew everybody's business and secrets. He told one piece of gossip after another and fancied himself as a real ladies' man. Harry said he was in bed with the flu when Dr. Bronner's family was killed.

When asked about Dr. Bronner, he stated the doctor was a wonderful man who didn't deserve to die like that. He went on to say Dr. Bronner didn't realize what a pack of wolves his top scientists were.

When asked to define wolves, he explained all of them wanted to be top dog and thought they should be the deputy CEO. He went on to say Dr. Newby was a real prick with a golden tongue who was a piss poor deputy CEO.

Tuesday afternoon, Byron went over to Mrs. Newby's home to conduct his interview. He pulled out the photo taken of the back of Dr. Newby's car at the accident scene, and asked Mrs. Newby if the damage was new.

She stated, "Agent, my husband's car was his baby; that damage was new, because he would never drive a car around dented like that."

Byron asked, "Did your husband take a briefcase to the conference?"

"Yes, he had a bunch of papers, folders, his laptop, medicine, and his cell phone in the briefcase."

"What was the medicine for?"

"He had a sinus infection, so his doctor gave him medicine for it."

"Do you have the briefcase, Mrs. Newby?"

"It's sitting on his desk, because I haven't felt like going through it."

"Would you let us check his cell phone and laptop just to make sure he wasn't receiving threats against his life?"

"You can take the briefcase, because I don't care."

"When did he last call you?"

"He called around 7:30 pm to let me know he was headed home ahead of the storm. I told him he might not get home before the storm, because it was coming in, quickly. I told him to wait until the storm was over, but he wouldn't listen to me."

"While we have been interviewing people at his work, several people have suggested your husband was having affairs with different co-workers. Is that true or just mean gossip?"

"My husband was a very handsome man, and women were always throwing themselves at him. I want you to understand my husband was no saint. We came to an agreement that if he had a fling, then, I was entitled to have a fling. If we ever reached a point where one or the other of us wanted out of the marriage, we would divorce and go our separate ways."

"Were you jealous over these flings?"

"If I got jealous every time a woman flirted with my husband, I'd be crazy by now."

"Did he ever ask you for a divorce?"

"No."

"Did you ask him for a divorce?"

"No."

"How long were you married?"

"We were married fourteen years."

"Was he paying child support to anyone?"

"Not that I know of, Agent. Before you ask, I've had two miscarriages and am unable to have children."

"Did your husband leave you with a mountain of debt?"

"No, my grandmother left me money and her home, and Duane had a million dollar life insurance policy with me as his beneficiary."

"How would you describe your marriage?"

"It was a marriage of convenience, we liked each other a lot, I was well provided for, our bills were paid, we enjoyed doing lots of things together, and we enjoyed sex."

"From our interviews, lots of people disliked your husband and said he shouldn't have been deputy CEO."

"Agent, I didn't get involved in his work or with the people he worked with. Dr. Bronner picked him to be deputy CEO, so I guess he knew Duane was qualified for the position. Maybe, these people were jealous of Duane."

"Do you know of anyone who might have wanted your husband dead?"

"You mean like killed? Heavens, no!"

Byron finished his interview, Mrs. Newby gave him her husband's briefcase with everything in it, and Byron left her his card in case she thought of something that might help the investigation. As he headed for Freestone, he shook his head and thought, "What a strange marriage those two had."

Agent Creekmore interviewed Dr. Stine's secretary and asked her if she had an affair with Dr. Newby.

She commented, "We had a brief fling, got tired of each other, and moved on."

"Did his wife find out about your affair?"

"It was my understanding she didn't care, because she had her own flings."

The secretary said she didn't like Zocrist and Harry Dent. In her opinion, Zocrist was an arrogant prick and strange. As far as Harry Dent was concerned, she said he fancied himself a ladies' man, but was a loser, instead. When Dr. Bronner and his family were murdered, she said she was working until 4:00 pm.

Detective Gage interviewed the female security guard who was supposed to have had an affair with Newby.

Her reply was, "I couldn't stand Dr. Newby, because he was an arrogant liar. I don't know where that gossip came from, but it's a lie! Besides, I'm happily married." She was off the day of the murders and couldn't understand why anyone would want to kill the family.

Detective Hansen found out that the girl in the IT

Department who Vernell Cleveland fired was now married to Dr. Stine's ex-husband. The present girl in the IT Department accused of having an affair with Newby told Hansen her live in boyfriend was the father of her baby, and they planned to get married in the summer. She stated, "I didn't have an affair with Newby or any other man at the company." When the murders occurred, she said she was working until 3:30 pm.

Late Tuesday afternoon, Task Force Bronner met in their conference room to go over the financial reports on all the major players at Bronner Pharmaceuticals. The whiz kids gave them information on all the people outside the major players the task force asked for.

Agent Sawyer gave Heather Dr. Newby's briefcase, so she could examine the cell phone and laptop. Detective Gage gave Heather a list of things he wanted Heather to look for.

Agents Creekmore and Donahue gave their cameras to Julie in the photo lab, so she could print photos of the memorials at Greta and Timmy's schools. Timmy might want to see them one day.

Tuesday, Art, Dolly, Ernesto, and Rosarita started decorating for Christmas. The men put both trees together and put the lights on. Dolly showed the men where she wanted the swags and wreaths put throughout the house. Rosarita put the flower arrangements around the house and wrapped the lighted garland around the spiral staircase.

While the ladies were putting the Christmas ornaments

on the trees, the men decorated the outside of the house with lights, bows, lighted angels, and lighted Christmas presents.

By the end of the day, all four were pooped out and ready for a good dinner. After they ate and cleaned up the kitchen, Ernesto and Rosarita went over to their cottage to relax. Art went upstairs to take a shower, and Dolly enjoyed a warm whirlpool bath. They crawled into their king size bed, cuddled, and read until they dropped off to sleep.

Wednesday, after they finished decorating the house, they planned to set back and enjoy their handiwork. Already, Art knew their home looked like a Christmas palace, and he had just as much fun decorating as Dolly did. This was a truly special Christmas coming for him and his gorgeous wife.

Tuesday evening, Cobra received a text message saying, "The wrong E. B., you idiot! Get it right!"

Cobra was pissed off about the message, because that meant Emily Bronner wasn't the target. *"Who worked at the company with the initials E. B.? Stay calm and think! I never make mistakes, so how could this have happened? How dare you call me an idiot! Yes, Dr. Stine's secretary's name is Emma Baker. I know where you live all by yourself in a little rambler about ten miles from the company. I'll pay you a visit to correct my little slip up, tonight."*

Cobra sent a text message back saying, "I'll take care of it."

Cobra walked up to the door, knocked, Emma looked through the peephole, and opened the door. *"I'm sorry, Emma. I've got car trouble and my cell phone is dead. Can I use your phone?"*

"Sure, it's right in here." Cobra knocked her to the floor, pulled out the gun, and pointed it at her head. She struggled with Cobra and knocked the gun on the floor. Both of them wrestled to reach the pistol as Emma dug her fingernails into Cobra's arm as they struggled to reach the pistol. Cobra grabbed the pistol, tried to aim it at Emma, but she was able to knock it away, again. *"Dammit, you witch! I'm going to blow your brains out!"* Cobra managed to hit Emma in the face causing her nose to bleed. With every ounce of energy she had left, Emma hit Cobra in the jaw and tried to reach the pistol. She got her hands on it, pointed it at Cobra, but when she pulled the trigger she missed.

As if in slow motion, Cobra wrestled the pistol away from her, took aim at her head, and fired. Emma felt as if lightning hit her head, and the pain was horrific. She saw stars, bright flashes of white and red lights. She felt like she was spinning into a dark deep hole which was so cold. Then, she felt like she was floating around and around in this dark hole. "How can I get out of this hole?"

Now, she felt like she was suspended in this deep hole. "Where am I?" She tried to get out of this hole, but her arms and legs wouldn't move. "Why am I here? Am I having a bad dream?" She tried to wake up to end this terrible dream, but she continued to float. All she could see were those flashes of white and red lights. "How can I be floating when I feel so heavy? I'm very tired, I need to rest, and I'm so weak."

Cobra rushed out the door, got into the car, and drove away. She didn't have neighbors close enough to hear the gunshots, but Cobra didn't want to take any chances. *"Witch, you scratched my arms with those darn fingernails. Well witch, I killed you anyway, so all that fighting didn't help you. At least, when I go into work, your scratches won't show, because my top will cover them. Goodbye, Emma Baker."*

"Hello Emma, my name is Becky, and I've come to help you. Don't go to sleep, because you must fight to stay alive. Fight the sleep, and talk to me, Emma."

Faintly, Emma heard a voice telling her to fight the sleep, but she was so tired. "I'm tired and I want to sleep."

"Don't sleep, Emma. You must stay awake, or you will die."

"Am I going to die?"

"You are a taker, Emma. If you want to live, you must be a giver."

"I want to live and not be selfish."

"I'm here to help bring you back."

"I can't see you, so where are you?"

"Look harder to see me, Emma."

"I'm trying, but all I see is a dark hole."

"Try harder, because help is on the way."

"I'm trying, but I'm so weak."

"Emma, look up towards the light. Can you see me?"

"You are a little girl with a cat."

"I've come to help you fight the sleep, if you want to live."

"I don't know you, and where am I?"

"You're on the floor in your living room, and I'm a friend. Keep looking at the light."

After Vince had lunch at the Deli, he took his coffee into his office. As he was sitting down, a picture flashed in his mind. He saw the letters E and B floating in the air. "Here we go, again. What does E and B mean, and how can this help me?"

Tuesday evening when Vince and Kris finished cleaning up the kitchen, they both took their coffee into the family room. He was telling Kris about his day when Becky appeared to both of them holding her cat.

"Emma needs help! She's lying on the floor in her house bleeding. She works at that company, and you must hurry!"

Vince called Detective Hansen and told him about his visions. Hansen looked through the company's roster and found an Emma Baker, and that was the only E and B on the list.

Vince said, "Hansen, get over to her house right away, because something is wrong."

When the police got there, they found Emma lying in a pool of blood on the living room carpet not far from the front door. The EMTs examined her, found a faint pulse, and when they took her blood pressure it was dangerously low. The ambulance rushed her to the emergency room where a trauma team was waiting. She was taken to surgery to repair the damage the bullet caused and to relieve the pressure on her brain.

Hansen was half way to the hospital when he got a call from the deputy sheriff at the hospital telling him what he knew, so far. He ordered the deputy to stay near her when she came out of surgery. Before coming to the hospital, he let the deputy know he was going to stop by the crime scene, first. Also, he told the deputy Freestone was sending a protection detail to guard her.

When Hansen ended his call, he got in touch with Vince to

tell him what he knew, so far. "Vince, have Chad put together a security detail for Emma in the hospital. When the killer finds out she's alive, the killer will come back to finish her off."

Vince asked, "Do you think she's Cobra's latest victim?"

"I'd bet money on it, but what I don't understand is why she was picked, because she's Dr. Stine's secretary not one of the major players headed up the corporate ladder."

Vince asked, "When the letters E and B flashed in my mind, they meant Emma Baker. Do the letters belong to someone else at the company?"

"Sweet Jesus! Those letters match Emily Bronner."

Vince asked, "Does anyone else have those initials in the company?"

"No, and I checked the list twice."

Hansen wondered out loud, "Could Cobra have killed the wrong woman?"

Vince replied, "The prick could have. Will the evidence from the crime scene be sent to us?"

"Yes, Sheriff Patterson said to send it to you."

Hansen told Vince he'd see him Wednesday once he checked the crime scene and found out Emma's condition after surgery.

When Hansen got to the hospital, he was directed to the intensive care waiting room until Emma was out of surgery.

He was thankful the techs found the bullet in the sofa, because that meant the surgeon didn't have to remove it from her brain.

Later, the surgeon came into the waiting room to talk to him, and he said, "Emma has a long gash on the left side of her head from the bullet. It caused a four inch fracture, so we had to relieve the pressure from the swelling. Her pulse and blood pressure are stable. Now, we have to wait until she comes out of her coma. Detective, she put up one hell of a fight, because she has a broken nose, several contusions, and several broken fingernails. Her clothes were bagged for the police, and you have my permission to collect evidence from under her fingernails."

"Was she sexually assaulted?"

"No."

"We know where she works and lives, so we'll try to find her next of kin and let the company know what has happened. She works for Bronner Pharmaceuticals, if you need to talk to them. Thank you for giving her a chance to live, because she can tell us what happened, and who did this to her."

The two shook hands, and Hansen went into intensive care to get the DNA evidence from under her fingernails. By looking at the poor woman, he knew she put up a fight which meant the attacker might be injured, too. Also, he let them know Freestone was sending a detail to guard her, because she was under witness protection, now.

As Hansen was leaving intensive care, a Freestone agent

walked up to him. He filled the agent in on the situation and Emma's condition. They shook hands; the agent relieved his deputy sheriff and took up his position.

Hansen headed back to Freestone with some more valuable evidence, and called Vince to update him concerning the surgeon's report.

Becky stayed with Emma to help her come out of her coma.

"Emma, keep looking at the light and fight the sleep."

"I'm trying to fight it, and I can see a little light."

"Look harder! Can you see me?"

"You're in a mist."

"Keep looking and the mist will fade away."

"Where am I, Becky."

"You're in the hospital getting lots of care."

"I feel so weak, but I'm not as cold."

"You are getting better, Emma."

"I feel so heavy, but I don't hurt."

"When you feel pain, you'll almost be back."

"Will you stay with me, Becky?"

"I'll be here when you need me."

"I'm afraid, Becky."

"Don't be afraid, because there are friends who are guarding you."

"I can see more light, and you are clearer, now."

"Just keep looking at the light, and you will get better."

"I want to live and change, Becky."

"Do you want to be a giver?"

"Yes, so give me another chance to make things right."

"Keep looking at the light, and I'll help you."

CHAPTER 8

Wednesday morning, Vince joined the task force to see how they were going to proceed, because of the attack on Emma Baker. The task force planned to get together and start going over interviews, and the printouts from the whiz kids, but Vince had a feeling that was going to change.

Hansen told the group about Emma Baker and said, "As of this morning, she is still in a coma. Her parents drove up from Portsmouth, Virginia and are at the hospital. I called Dr. Lim with the news and told him the task force will be there to conduct more interviews, shortly."

Hansen looked at Ryan and said, "Make sure you interview Dr. Newby's secretary, today. Look for anyone who has injuries consistent with the attack last night.

Hansen told Brad, "Make sure you interview Dr. Zocrist's secretary, too. Also, look for those injuries."

Hansen told Byron to do the same thing concerning Dr. Harris' secretary.

Detective Gage spoke up and continued, "I'm interviewing the security employees that work for Harry Dent, and all the employees in the cafeteria."

Ryan spoke up and added, "I ate lunch there Monday, and a note was slipped under my plate. It said to check out the serious argument between Dr. Zocrist and Dr. Tanner the day Dr. Newby was killed.

Hansen replied, "Talk to Tanner about that issue, and Brad can ask Zocrist about it. I'm interviewing the rest of the employees in the IT Department, shipping and receiving, and the finance office. Make sure you ask everyone where they were last night between 7:00 pm and 8:30 pm."

Gage asked Vince, "Can you have Jason and Shontelle go through the financial reports on the Bronner employees and highlight any red flags for us?"

"Sure, we can do that for you, plus I'll help them after I finish with Team 8."

Brad asked, "Do we know anything about the funeral services?"

Vince answered, "Dolly and Art are going to a funeral home on Friday to make arrangements, and she'll let us know as soon as possible."

Vince was very pleased with Team 8 concerning their Justice Department case. Even though it was a sad ending, they were able to bring the case to a successful conclusion. All they had to do was finish up the paperwork and enjoy a week's vacation. Since both agents were married, they decided to take their families to Disney World the day after Thanksgiving. Team 8 would be back on December 3rd, so Vince decided to give them the missing person's case.

When Vince was finished with Team 8, Freestone's Supervisor of Safe House Security, Walt Hensley walked into Vince's office with a very distinguished looking man with

Native American features. Walt introduced him as Mitchell Raven, and the men shook hands.

Walt said, "Mitch and I have looked over the stone farmhouse and Millie's property. He agrees the barn will make a perfect nerve center, and the plan I have for Millie's place will secure it."

"So, Walt convinced you to join our ranks?"

Mitch replied, "Freestone is a top notch organization, and I'm pleased to be a part of it. Walt has called in some more people he knows to speed up construction and security upgrades at the two properties."

Vince added, "Dolly wants Millie's place finished as soon as possible followed by the stone farmhouse."

Walt followed with, "Millie's area will be finished the second week in December. Every inch of her area will be covered, and when the nerve center is done we can hook her up to our bank of computers."

Vince asked, "Do you have an idea about when the nerve center will be ready for business?"

Mitch answered, "I'm thinking it will be ready to hook up with all your safe houses by mid-January depending on the weather."

"Is the stone farmhouse itself ready to be a safe house with security agents if we need it?"

Walt answered, "Yes, you just won't have all the bells and whistles available until the nerve center is complete."

"Have you two sat down with the 3M ladies to explain everything you are doing?"

Walt remarked, "We're headed their way after lunch, because I want Mitch to sample the Deli's delicious menu, first, before we tackle Ms. Mabel."

Vince added with a smile, "Both of you better hold on to your britches and be ready for anything."

All the men laughed, because Walt told Mitch all about Mabel at the cookout, the card he sent her, and the pumpkin bracelet. Walt planned to give Mabel a silly Christmas bracelet just to get her riled up good and proper.

Mitch asked, "I understand your forensic scientist has Native American roots to the Cherokee Nation in western North Carolina. Can I meet her?"

"Sure, I'll introduce you to her, and then we can have lunch at the Deli."

Heather and Mitch had a pleasant visit, and Vince knew she appreciated the gesture of respect from another Native American whose roots were connected to the Navajo Nation.

The task force continued to interview Bronner employees who were shocked when they heard about the attack on Emma Baker.

However, one employee was furious, because Cobra couldn't believe the witch was still alive. *"How can I finish her off without the entire police department coming down on me like a hammer? I need to stay calm, because an idea will present itself in due time."*

Agent Creekmore's interview with Dr. Newby's secretary produced some good clues. She knew her boss was a jerk, ran after women, and she added, "Agent, I'm thirty-eight years old and black. Dr. Newby ran after young white women, so I didn't have to worry about him putting the make on me." She did tell the agent Dr. Newby had several arguments with Dr. Zocrist, because the men never agreed on anything.

Agent Donahue's interview with Dr. Zocrist's secretary confirmed Newby and Zocrist never got along, and Maria Santana was a frequent visitor to Zocrist's office for some tender loving care.

When Brad asked Zocrist about his argument with Dr. Tanner, he said it was about money Tanner owed him. Zocrist stated, "The prick was too slow paying back the $500.00 he borrowed from me."

Agent Sawyer's interview with Dr. Harris' secretary didn't produce much information, because she had only worked at the company for a year. She liked Dr. Harris and concentrated on doing a good job.

When Agent Creekmore asked Tanner, senior scientist in the Production Division, about his argument with Zocrist he said, "I was paying the money back $100.00 a paycheck, but he went ballistic on me for being too slow. The man agreed to the payment plan in the beginning, but all of a sudden he demanded all of it. If you ask me, Zocrist, Stine, and Harris are all jackasses, and Newby was the number one jackass."

Task Force Bronner finished up most of their interviews and headed back to Freestone. They agreed to enjoy Thanksgiving with their loved ones and meet back at Freestone Friday to start going over all the printouts, evidence reports from Heather, and all the information they gathered from their interviews.

Walt and Mitch stopped by Millie's place to go over the plans for her place, and the stone farmhouse property including the barn nerve center. The 3M ladies were very impressed and thankful Walt called in more crews to finish the work sooner.

Millie asked, "Since you had to move, where are you staying, Mitch?"

"I'm staying with Walt, and Dolly has invited me to enjoy Thanksgiving at their home."

Millie continued, "Where do you plan to live?"

"I'd like to find a home around here to buy, because I don't like apartments or townhouses."

Millie added, "Ask Dolly about the place she knows that is vacate."

"Thanks for telling me; I'll do that."

Mabel spoke up and added, "Since you are part of Freestone, you better do an excellent job for Dolly, or she'll tie your ears together."

Walt answered, "She'll get the best from us, but we're more worried about what you three ladies will do to us, if we mess up."

Mabel shot back, "Walt, we'll turn you into potted meat and Mitch into a teepee."

Mitch replied, "Don't worry ladies; you'll get our A game."

Mandy asked, "Mitch, where are your Native American roots from?"

"Mine come from the Navajo Nation."

Timmy popped out from nowhere and said, "Your people were code talkers during World War II."

Mitch looked surprised and said, "You're right, little guy."

Timmy stared at Mitch for a moment, put his finger on Mitch's forehead and said, "You have the sight, but you don't trust it."

Mitch blinked several times and asked, "You can see?"

"I can see and you know it, but you don't trust."

Millie and Sheridan proceeded to tell Mitch about their encounters with Becky as he sat stunned. Timmy put his hands on his hips and said, "Sheridan trusted Becky, and she helped her escape. I trusted Becky, and she led me here. Vince trusts even though he is impatient."

Walt looked at Timmy and asked, "Do I see?"

"No sir, you don't have that sense."

Mabel piped in, "I'm glad I don't have the sense, because I don't want my three dead husbands to pester the crap out of me and turn me into a basket case."

Millie shot back, "You've been a basket case since we were kids, sister dear."

Mabel fumed, "You've been a Halloween ghost all your life, sister dear."

Mandy added, "When you two pass on, don't come back and pester me to death, please."

Adam chimed in, "When you two ladies pass on, don't send Greedy Gut back to pester me to death, either."

Erika piped in, "Don't send all those fat ass chipmunks to pester me from chipmunk heaven, please."

Sheridan jumped in, "Please, don't send all those fat shitty birds to pester me from bird heaven. I don't want bird shit messing up my hairdo."

By then, there was laughing chaos throughout the house including Timmy who was rolling on the floor holding his stomach. Finally, he got off the floor, looked at Mabel and asked, "Will you pester me with your pepper blaster and bunny rabbit slippers?"

Mabel answered, "You can bet on it, Timbo."

Pixie and Dixie thought, "We're going to doggy heaven and pester Mabel with our fleas."

The little tike fell on the floor laughing as Pixie and Dixie played with him.

Mitch thought, "Are these people wonderful, or are they just plain crazy?"

Walt asked, "Mabel, have you been line dancing, yet?"

"No, I'm too old for that crap, and I told you that before. Don't you understand English?"

Walt stated, "I guess I'll have to hog tie you, dump you in my car, and carry you there under protest."

Millie piped in, "I'd love to see you hog tie Mabel."

Mabel shot back, "You can't hog tie me, because I possess lightning moves, Weasel!"

Walt countered, "Show me those lightning moves line dancing."

Mabel shouted, "Time out here! You're making me dizzy!"

Millie fired back, "You have always been dizzy, sister dear."

Pixie and Dixie looked at each other and thought, "All these crazy people are making us dizzy."

Mabel threw up her hands, stomped out on the deck, paced, and mumbled to herself.

Mandy added, "Walt, I think you got in the last word."

He said, "I think this requires a peace offering from me."

Mitch added, "I think you better, Boss."

All eyes followed Walt to the deck to see what Mabel was going to do next. She'd probably hog tie him upside down on the grill.

"I thought you might like this to throw in the trash."

Mabel opened the box, saw the silly Christmas bracelet, and said, "Thank you. It's cute and I like it, but I don't know whether to deck your behind or feed you to Millie's wild kingdom."

"So, you want to turn me into bird seed, Pumpkin."

Mabel stomped upstairs to her room and closed the door as Walt howled with laughter.

Millie chimed in, "She's laughing herself silly, putting the box in her dresser, freshening up her make up, and she'll come down to start dinner, shortly."

Sure enough, that's what Mabel did. Of course, she made sure Walt and Mitch were staying for dinner.

The entire group laughed, visited, and enjoyed a fantastic meal together. Mandy was amazed at how easily Timbo was able to talk to everyone and catch the meaning to the jokes flying back and forth. Sometimes, the boy's intelligence scared her, but she didn't know why.

Walt looked at Adam and Mandy saying, "Congratulations, I hear you two are getting married December 19th."

Mandy blushed and Adam thanked Walt and told him he was looking forward to working with Mitch and him at the stone farmhouse property.

Millie added, "When you get married, I hope the stone farmhouse will be ready to move into along with Timbo and the security detail."

Walt answered, "We'll make sure it happens."

Timbo asked, "Can I come back and visit everybody?"

Mabel replied, "Of course, you can, honey. Pixie and Dixie will want to see you, too."

"I'm going to miss them something awful."

Adam commented, "When we move into the stone farmhouse, I guess we better get you a dog."

"I can have my very own dog?"

"Sure, what kind do you want?"

"I'd like a dog like Pixie and Dixie or a Labrador."

"Okay, it's settled then. What are you going to name her or him?"

"I don't know, because I have to think on it a bit."

The ladies cleared the table after everybody finished their dessert. Mabel was a good girl and passed on the German chocolate cake.

Walt asked, "How is your diet coming along, Mabel?"

Mabel fumed, "That quack doctor has no idea how hard it has been to lose only nine pounds. I still have six more pounds to lose, but I'm frustrated. Those six pounds are going to kill me, because I know I won't lose them with the holidays coming. I'm craving a piece of pumpkin pie, already."

Walt shot back, "I'm telling you, you'd enjoy line dancing and lose weight at the same time."

Adam piped in, "Mandy, put some music on, so we can show Mabel some moves."

Everyone went into the family room, Mandy put the music on, and Adam and Mandy started dancing. It wasn't long before Walt and Millie joined in.

Mandy said, "Come on and join us, Timbo."

He watched a little longer, and then joined in not missing a step. He clapped his hands as the group really got into the swing of things. Timbo added some moves of his own and Walt asked, "I like that. Will you show me how to do it?" It wasn't long before everybody was picking up on Timbo's added moves.

Sheridan clapped and said, "When I get out of this cast, I'm learning how to line dance."

Cody added, "I'll take you dancing any time you want."

Erika clapped and said, "I'm with you, Sheridan. This is a great way for us to get back in shape."

Timbo looked at Mabel and asked, "Don't you feel the music in your body, Aunt Mabel? I know you feel it when you play the piano, just like me."

Walt pulled Mabel out of her chair and said, "That's it! If Timbo can do it, so can you. Now, stand by Timbo and follow his lead. No more excuses, Mabel."

All of a sudden, it was as if only Mabel and Timbo were line dancing. The two picked up on the rhythm and fell in sync with each other. The two looked at each other and smiled as Mabel kept up with Timbo's every move. Walt moved in beside Mabel as the group kept dancing with the music. Adam and Mandy couldn't believe their eyes as Walt, Mabel, Millie, and Timbo moved in perfect rhythm with the music and each other. After thirty minutes, the group decided to take a break and get something to drink.

Timbo said, "I knew you could do it Aunt Millie and Aunt Mabel."

Millie replied, "That was fantastic! Gil and I are going to do this every week. This is a lot of fun."

Adam added, "Everybody was great! Where did you learn to line dance, Timbo?"

"I learned how to do it, tonight."

Mitch said, "Well, you looked like a pro to me."

Walt looked at Mabel and said, "You did great, Mabel! What's best of all is we burned up a lot of calories, too."

Mabel shot back, "I felt like a hippo bouncing around out

there, and I burned up two calories, probably."

Walt fired back, "You are not a hippo, and I know you enjoyed it!"

Millie chimed in, "You only looked like a small elephant, sister dear."

Mabel shot back, "You looked like a monkey swinging around, sister dear."

Walt added, "I felt like a baboon jumping around."

Adam remarked, "I felt like a walrus sliding around."

Mandy replied, "I felt like Greedy Gut racing across the yard."

Erika asked, "What did you feel like, Timbo?"

Timbo put his hands on his hips and answered, "I felt like an eagle soaring across the sky, sister dear."

The whole crowd broke out in waves of laughter, because Timbo had sister dear down pat right down to the hip movement.

Mabel looked at everybody and said, "I did enjoy it, and it's very good exercise. I have to admit Timbo is a great teacher. There might be something to this line dancing after all. At least, I didn't break my hip."

The friends visited for a while longer, then said their goodbyes. Walt hugged Millie, Mandy, Erika, and Sheridan goodbye. When he got to Mabel he put his hand out and asked, "Do you want to kiss my hand?"

Mabel fired back, "Are you nuts! I don't want rabies."

Walt grabbed her hand, pulled her towards him, and kissed her forehead.

Millie shouted, "You better wash your forehead before you catch his rabies, sister dear."

Walt and Mitch laughed as they walked to their car. On the way home, Mitch commented, "I've never had a day like this one in my entire life, and that Mabel is one crazy, delightful woman. Too bad she's old enough to be my mother, because I'd fight you for her charms."

Walt replied, "Yep, Mabel can sure get one's blood boiling, and I've never met a woman like her, either. Sometimes, I don't know whether to kiss her or smack her. One thing for sure, if I smacked her, she'd punch my lights out."

Mitch laughed and added, "I guess you better kiss her, so she won't beat you up."

Both men laughed and let their thoughts wander to Thanksgiving Day at Art and Dolly's home.

Mitch let his thoughts wander to the conversation he had with Timbo. "Is the little boy right? Maybe, I don't trust what I see or hear.

CHAPTER 9

This was the best Thanksgiving Day Art ever experienced. His children and grandchildren were blown away at how gorgeous their home was decorated. Dolly had each grandchild's name painted on a beautiful Christmas ornament, so each could put theirs on one of the Christmas trees. Even his son, daughter-in-law, daughter, and son-in-law were given their ornaments to put on the trees.

All of Art's family told Dolly they felt like they were in a Christmas wonderland fit for a king. Also, Dolly gave the families beautiful ornaments to take home for their own trees. The expressions Art saw on his families' faces were well worth the honeymoon trip to Pigeon Forge.

Rosarita and Dolly put together a fantastic holiday feast with all the trimmings. Everyone couldn't believe the ham wasn't salty, so lots of folks ate another slice. Art looked at his grandchildren and couldn't believe how much food they could eat and still have room for dessert. The desserts were a big hit, because there wasn't any left when the meal was over.

Desiree and Tom Hansen were stunned at how beautiful the house looked, and they were surprised when Dolly gave them some ornaments and a gorgeous wreath for Desiree's front door.

Desiree had to tell Art and Dolly what went on at Freestone when Nathan Donovan and his family visited. Everyone howled with laughter over Sierra's reaction to

Nathan and all the teasing that went on. Dolly and Art thought, "Do we have another romance on the horizon?"

Walt looked around the home and dinner table and thought, "This is what I miss the most since my wife died. All these folks are such wonderful loving people to be around." He told them about Mabel dancing and about her reaction to the silly bracelet. He thought he might have to pick Dolly, Art, and Desiree off the floor they were laughing so hard.

Mitch had never experienced a Thanksgiving like this one, so he was enjoying every minute of it and the food.

Art's grandchildren were very interested in his Navajo Nation roots, and they asked him lots of questions about their traditions.

Mitch asked about the vacant home Millie mentioned, so Dolly told him its history, and invited Walt and him to help the group move things out of the house on Sunday. That way Mitch could get a good look around and help out at the same time.

Art showed him their classic cars, and he was more than impressed. He loved old cars, so he told Art he was very interested in buying one himself. Mitch told Art what cars he was partial to, so Art suggested he go to the next show and put some feelers out for what he wanted.

After everyone left to head for home, Art and Dolly put their special ornaments on the tree in the family room and toasted each other with hot chocolate.

Proudly, Art told Dolly how extra special this Thanksgiving was for him and his family.

Thanksgiving at Millie's farmhouse was extra special for Sierra, Sheridan, Erika, Adam, Cody, and Timbo. None of them could believe what a feast the 3M ladies put on the table. Everybody feasted until they were ready to pop including Timbo. The ladies knew one thing for sure; Timbo loved mashed potatoes and pumpkin pie.

Sierra and Sheridan never had a holiday like this one, because their father was such a heartless prick. Both women prayed they would have a lot more special days like this one.

Millie looked at Sheridan and Cody and sensed some electricity flowing between them. She thought, "Is there another romance starting to bud?"

Dan was spending a lot of time around Erika, as they talked and laughed oblivious to the rest of the folks around them.

Millie hoped Dan would find a special woman to love after his disastrous marriage and nasty divorce.

Byron looked at his father and knew the two of them wanted to experience holidays like this one for many years to come.

Mandy and Adam put some music on to dance to, so Millie could show Gil how much fun it was. Before the evening was over, Timbo had Gil, Byron, Cody, and Dan following his lead in sync with one another. Of course, Timbo had to add some more special moves of his own that everybody needed to learn.

Once the dancing was over, Mandy asked Timbo to play the piano for everyone. Byron and Gil had no idea how talented this little boy was. They felt like they had gone to a concert at the Kennedy Center in Washington, D. C. The two men sat with their mouths wide open as they watched Timbo play.

When it came time to head back home, the folks said their goodbyes knowing Timbo was treated to an extra special Thanksgiving.

Isa, the night nurse, came in to get her two patients ready for bed, and Mandy took Timbo upstairs to get his bath.

Mandy knew it wasn't going to be too long before Timbo fell asleep, because he had one busy, delightful day. She said to herself, "Emily Bronner, I promise you we'll love and keep him safe. I just wanted you to know in case you can read my thoughts."

Becky stayed with Emma to keep her from slipping away.

"Emma, can you hear me?"

"Yes, I'm still looking at the light."

"You are getting better, but remember you must look at the light."

"What happened to me?"

"You were shot in the head."

"Why was I shot?"

"Someone wanted to kill you."

"Who tried to kill me?"

"A person you work with."

"What is the person's name?"

"I don't know, but you'll remember, later on."

"Why does this person want to kill me?"

"This evil person takes and never gives."

Friday morning, Art and Dolly met with the funeral home director, so they could make arrangements for the private burial of Timmy's family. She let the director know there would be a memorial service at the Bronner's church starting at 7:00 pm, Monday evening.

When Art and Dolly left the funeral home, they headed for the Bronner property in Rappahannock County. When they pulled up to the cabin, it was obvious Dr. Bronner bought the five acres to build a new cabin on. The existing cabin was little more than a shack.

Art said, "If a new cabin was built on the property, it would be beautiful. We could build a nice cabin here, so Mandy, Adam, and Timmy could have a perfect getaway place in the mountains. What do you think, Lady Bug?"

"It sounds wonderful to me. We can start building the cabin home as a surprise for the three of them. Let's hope it'll be finished come spring or summer."

"That's settled then, so let's head home to enjoy our Christmas Palace."

After having Thanksgiving at a friend's house, Cobra was going to spend the next three days at a getaway cabin near Front Royal away from everybody. *"So what, if the witch is in a coma in the hospital under guard, I have time to figure something out to get rid of her. I'll get my money and then head to Mexico to hide out and live like royalty. I'm not going to share the money with anyone. I won't have to put up with that rattlesnake's nest full of weird, arrogant scientists."*

Friday morning, Cobra pulled up to the cabin and unloaded the groceries. The killer got a good fire started in the stove and went outdoors to bring in more firewood. Cobra decided to cut up some firewood and fix the cover over the dry well before calling it a day. The firewood was put near the shed to season, and Cobra cut some pieces of lumber to replace the rotten ones covering the well. As the killer was getting ready to nail a plank down, Cobra was pushed from behind, and crashed through the rotten planks.

Frantically, Cobra tried to break the fall, but it was too late. The killer hit the rocky bottom into nothingness.

Task Force Bronner met at Freestone at 10:00 am Friday to start plowing through all the information collected, so far. First, everyone looked at Heather's reports she left them from the autopsies and evidence. All three members of the Bronner family were killed with the same .22 caliber pistol, and there were no matches when she ran it through all the databases.

The shoe print found near the shed didn't match Dr. Bronner's size ten, because the Nike tennis shoe was a size twelve. Heather was able to get DNA from under Mrs. Bronner's fingernails and from hairs on her blouse that didn't match any family member. Of course, she was waiting for the DNA profiles to be processed.

Heather was processing the DNA found under Emma Baker's fingernails, and the weapon used to shoot her was a .22 caliber pistol.

Dr. Newby's cell phone contained calls back and forth to his work, colleagues, secretary, and wife. The last call made was to his wife on the day that he was killed. Heather found no threatening messages sent or received on his cell phone or laptop. Information on his laptop pertained to his work or the conference he attended in Washington, D. C. There was nothing on his laptop or cell phone to suggest he was having an affair.

Detective Gage looked at the team and said, "Bronner's company is a hotbed of jealousy, hatred, affairs, and pissed off egos. Now, we have an attempted murder involving Emma Baker who is Dr. Stine's secretary."

Hansen spoke up and added, "Emma is still in a coma, but she's showing signs of improvement. I want to throw an idea on the table, because I want your feedback. Mrs. Bronner's initials are E and B, and we have Emma Baker with the same initials. Could the killer have murdered the wrong person?"

Ryan replied, "It's possible. Do any more people at this company have the same initials?"

"No, and I went through that list twice."

Brad answered, "I agree with Ryan, because the people in this company are capable of just about anything, in my opinion."

Byron added, "I'd say it is quite possible, because there's some weird ducks working there."

Detective Gage said, "First, let's start with Dr. Newby. Just about everybody hated or disliked him. He stole ideas from his colleagues, had affairs at work, and Emma Baker admitted to an affair saying they had a fling and then moved on. According to Mrs. Newby, she knew he had flings, so she had her own flings."

"Second, Dr. Zocrist isn't well liked, he hated Newby, he had a problem over money with Dr. Tanner, he was upset Dr. Lim was hired, and is supposed to have the hots for Maria

Santana and Dr. Beach."

"Third, we have Dr. Stine who isn't well liked; she hated Newby, and was upset Dr. Lim was hired."

"Fourth, Dr. Harris seems to be liked, he hated Newby, and was upset Dr. Lim was hired."

Gage added, "The day of the murders Dr. Stine and Dr. Harris left work at 4:30 pm, and Dr. Zocrist had a dentist appointment at 11:00 am. I want to repeat the fact that this scenario could be an ordered hit, so just because someone is at work doesn't cross them off the suspect's list."

Hansen said, "Let's look at Maria Santana who is glad Newby is dead and is supposed to have the hots for Dr. Zocrist and Harry Dent, our super stud head of security. She was home with a sinus infection the day of the murders."

"Next, we have Hansa Fareed who loved Dr. Bronner, babysat his children on occasion, and left work at 2:00 pm with female issues the day of the murders."

"Next, we have Dillon Carr who disliked Newby and all the white coats, because they were arrogant and jealous of one another. He agreed with the hiring of Dr. Lim and was home sick with the flu during the murders."

"Next, we have Vernell Cleveland who was in a meeting with Dr. Lim until 5:00 pm. Also, she stated Maria Santana had the hots for Zocrist, Harry Dent, Dillon Carr, Jesse Rice, and Dr. Tanner. I guess Maria likes variety to spice up her life."

"Next, we have Harry Dent who is mostly disliked, said to

be arrogant, called the top scientists a pack of wolves, considered himself a ladies' man, and was home sick with the flu during the murders."

"Lastly, we have Jesse Rice who disliked the white coats calling them arrogant and strange; he liked Dr. Bronner, and was another flu victim at home during the murders."

Gage looked at Byron and asked, "Was the damage new to the rear bumper to Dr. Newby's car?"

"Yes, because his wife said Duane would never drive a car with that kind of damage."

Gage asked, "Was Mrs. Newby aware of her husband's affairs?"

"Yes, she said they had an agreement about his flings, and if one wanted out of the marriage they would divorce and go their separate ways."

Ryan commented, "Shit, that's one strange marriage, as far as I'm concerned."

"She called it a marriage of convenience."

Brad remarked, "You said she inherited a lot of money from her grandmother, and she got her husband's million dollar life insurance pay off."

"Yes, so that makes her a wealthy widow."

Ryan added, "She could be a black widow, too. She could have gotten fed up with her husband's affairs and ran him off the road or had someone else do it."

Brad remarked, "There are several people on our list who could have run Newby off the road."

Hansen said, "Our three main management scientists on the corporate ladder are Stine, Zocrist, and Harris. All three were pissed, because they weren't promoted. The best suspect is Zocrist, because his dentist appointment didn't last all day. The other two would need someone else to do the dirty work."

Byron continued, "The senior scientist of the Research Division, Dr. Clara Beach, disliked Newby and Stine calling them gold diggers. She agreed with the hiring of Dr. Lim and said Harry Dent thought he was a super stud. The day of the murders she worked until 4:30 pm."

"The senior scientist of the Testing Division, Dr. Rose Smith, said Newby was a prick who tried to put the make on her. Also, she agreed with the hiring of Dr. Lim, because there was too much jealousy whirling around the top candidates. On the day of the murders, she left work at 3:00 pm."

"The senior scientist of the Production Division, Dr. Roy Tanner hated Newby, Zocrist, and Stine. He had a nasty run in with Zocrist over borrowed money, and he agreed with the hiring of Dr. Lim. The rumor mill has him dating Maria Santana, Dr. Beach, and the widow Mrs. Newby. He was another flu victim at home during the murders."

Hansen added, "Here's some feedback from my interviews in the IT Department, finance, and the shipping department.

These areas are a regular rollercoaster ride through Gossip Mountain. Dr. Newby put the make on just about every female employee no matter what department they worked in."

"Harry Dent dated Maria Santana, Hansa Fareed, Emma Baker, and several women in the cafeteria.

Jesse Rice dated Hansa Fareed, Emma Baker, a woman in finance, a woman in the IT Department, and several women who worked in production. One rumor has him dating Mrs. Newby."

"Dillon Carr dated Maria Santana, Hansa Fareed, Emma Baker, a woman in testing, and the now available, Mrs. Newby."

"Another rumor has Dr. Stine going hot and heavy with Dillon Carr and Harry Dent. I don't mind telling you guys this gossip mill has my head spinning."

Detective Gage added, "I ran into the same gossip mill when talking to the cafeteria workers. I don't know how they could get any work done while they jumped from one bed to the next one at this company."

Ryan asked, "Do we go back to the people on the rumor mill and ask them point blank if they were seeing these people?"

Gage replied, "Yes, because we don't have any other choice, but to weed through the gossip to find out the truth. Someone out there is pissed off enough to commit murder or have someone else do the dirty work for them."

Brad remarked, "I'm frustrated, because the suspect list is endless and nobody really jumps off the page at me."

Ryan added, "Shit, I feel like I'm stuck in quicksand."

Byron commented, "I'm looking at Emma Baker and asking myself what does Emma, Newby, and Dr. Bronner's family have in common other than Bronner Pharmaceuticals? Emma had an affair with Newby, and she shares the same initials as Emily Bronner. Someone didn't like her affair with Newby, and Hansen might be right about Emily being murdered by mistake."

Ryan remarked, "Then, you're thinking we have a killer, and the person who ordered the hit."

Gage asked, "Wouldn't the killer know the difference between Emily and Emma?"

Brad answered, "If the killer is from outside the company, the mistake could have been possible."

Byron continued, "The person who ordered the killing is connected to the company, and my gut tells me Dr. Newby was the first victim."

Hansen said, "One thing for sure, Dr. Newby pissed off someone enough to have him murdered. Our only problem is Newby was hated or disliked by almost everyone that worked at the company, so the suspect list is still ten miles long."

Ryan remarked, "Newby chased after almost every

woman who worked at the company who wasn't black, so that still leaves us with a suspect list eight miles long."

Brad replied, "At this point, I'm not ruling out anyone male or female."

Hansen commented, "I hope Emma wakes up soon, so she can tell us who attacked her."

Gage stated, "I'm meeting with Dr. Lim and Judge Franklin on Saturday to discuss how the company will be run until this case is resolved."

"Byron is meeting with the Bronner's minister on Saturday to go over our security plan for the memorial service. We'll all be there to observe the mourners."

"Ryan is meeting with Mr. and Mrs. Madison who were close friends of the Bronner's through their church."

"Brad is meeting with Mr. and Mrs. Vogel who were close friends of the Bronner's."

"Hansen is going to see Emma in the hospital and talk to her parents."

Gage added, "We can talk this to death, but we don't have enough clues, yet. Let's keep talking to people and running down leads. I have a feeling the memorial service will provide us with more clues."

Sunday, Gage met Art, Dolly, and their helpers at the Bronner home to move more things over to the stone farmhouse. This time, Mandy came along, so she could pick out items that could be used at the farmhouse. When Mitch Raven saw the home and its property, he loved it. Dolly told him she would contact a realtor to give her an idea how much this home was worth on the open market. Then, they could sit down and discuss the sale of the home. Mitch told Dolly he was willing to pay more just to make sure she'd sell it to him.

The group's number one priority this time was to move the piano, the rest of Timmy's clothes, two bedroom suites, and the formal dining room table, chairs, and china cabinet. Mandy was tickled to death to get the china and crystal in the cabinet. She went around and picked out her favorite lamps, pictures, books, and reminded everyone about Christmas decorations. They found the Christmas things stored in the basement in a room by themselves, because the attic wasn't big enough to cuss a cat in.

Dolly told Gage about the church needing the Bronner clothing, so Gage told her to load those things in his truck, and he would take them to the church Monday evening before the memorial service.

Once everything was loaded up, the caravan headed for the stone farmhouse to unload all the furniture, china, and crystal. After the group put away all the items, they were ready to call it a day and enjoy dinner at a local restaurant. They didn't want to pile in on Millie and Mabel every time they were in the area, so that's why they chose to eat out. Also, they wanted to treat Mandy to a meal out in town, because she'd helped to feed them enough.

They enjoyed a wonderful meal together and left for

home, because tomorrow was back to work for most everyone including Dolly.

CHAPTER 10

Monday morning, Director Dolly Hamilton walked into Freestone on her first day back since her surgery and said, "Good morning, how is my kindergarten class, today?"

Shontelle jumped up from her desk and asked, "Ms. Dolly, did I just hear you call us your kindergarten class?"

"That's right, Shontelle."

Shontelle fired back, "Well, I have you to know I graduated from high school, and I have a college degree, missy."

"Yes, but you are still in my kindergarten class."

Jason asked, "Ms. Dolly, are you sure you're able to come back to work?"

"I'm just fine, Jason."

Sierra piped in, "Ms. Dolly, I know what happened to you. You swallowed one of Greedy Gut's peanut butter crackers, and it's turned your brain to fluff."

"My brain is fine, and you're still in my kindergarten class, too."

Shontelle fired back, "Lord, I better call Desiree and have her come and slap the crap out of you, because you've gone crazy."

"Desiree is in the class with you."

Jason chimed in, "Lord, don't tell me you're going to throw bull around here like Vince."

Shontelle shot back, "Vince throws enough bull around here to turn the walls brown. You cannot throw bull around, missy!"

Sierra chimed in, "We don't have enough buckets and shovels to scoop your bull up, too."

"Well, I guess you better clean the walls and get more buckets and shovels."

Just then, Vince walked up with a cup of coffee.

Shontelle said, "This is your fault, Hollywood."

"What did I do?"

Jason replied, "You turned Ms. Dolly into a smart butt like you. She's turned into you."

"Oh no, don't you blame me for whatever she's doing."

Diana piped in, "Oh yes it is! You turned Ms. Dolly to the dark side and burned up her brain."

Dolly turned to Vince and said, "Just what I thought; the whole office is in kindergarten."

Vince added, "Don't pull me into this, because I'm still in nursery school."

Jason fired back, "Dang, I feel like I'm in a nuthouse."

Dolly couldn't help herself, so she burst out laughing until tears ran down her cheeks. Shontelle was laughing so hard she fell off her chair. Sierra laughed until she had to run to the bathroom, and Jason laughed so hard he started having cramps in his sides.

Vince looked at Dolly and said, "Welcome back general, the nuthouse is still screwed up as usual."

The two walked towards their offices and Dolly said, "That felt real good, Vince."

"That's Looney Tune Land at Freestone, for you."

Shontelle shouted, "Don't start throwing manure pies around here, because we've got work to do, you two."

Desiree walked through, stopped, and asked, "Whose throwing manure pies?"

Shontelle chimed back, "Hollywood and that crazy cousin of yours."

Desiree looked puzzled and asked, "You mean Dolly's throwing manure pies?"

Shontelle replied, "Desiree, you only have one cousin, bonehead."

"I better take her temperature to see if she's sick."

Diana piped in, "Desiree, it's too late. Dolly has crossed over into buffalo chip land, forever."

Desiree shot back, "If that's the case, then I need to slap the crap out of her big time!"

Sierra shouted, "You go girl!"

Vince and Dolly heard this exchange, went into Dolly's office, and howled until they hurt. Desiree went into Dolly's office, saw what was happening, put a pile of papers on Dolly's desk and said, "It's about time you loosened up your girdle, Ms. Bad Butt Lawyer."

"I don't have a girdle on."

"Good!"

All three laughed themselves under the carpet, and all Vince could do was hand out Kleenex. Finally, when they calmed down, Dolly asked Vince if David gave Heather her engagement ring over the holiday.

"Dolly, I was proud of him, because he gave Heather her ring right in front of her parents. Of course, Heather turned ten shades of red, but her parents hugged and kissed both of them silly. It's safe to say her family loves David a great deal. The families sat down with the happy couple, and everyone decided August 21st would be a perfect wedding date. David has already asked me to be his best man, and his ushers will be Jason, Eric, and Nathan."

Dolly commented and asked, "I'll pay Heather a surprise visit to see her ring. Speaking of Nathan, wasn't he supposed to call Sierra this weekend?"

Desiree spoke up and said, "That's right! I can't resist this, so let's go back out there and find out what happened. Vince, he did call her, right?"

"Oh yes!"

The three walked back out to the work station area and stopped at Sierra's console. The poor girl had no idea what was coming as she looked up at them and asked, "Did I do something wrong, Ms. Dolly?"

"Well now, that all depends on whether you spent Saturday and Sunday nights in a motel."

"Why on earth would I do that, Ms. Dolly?"

"So, you weren't lusting under the sheets?"

"What would I be lusting about?"

Desiree piped in and asked, "You mean you spent those two nights in your apartment?"

"Of course, I did, Ms. Desiree!"

Dolly asked, "Did you get a phone call from a male you had a picture taken with this weekend?"

"Yes I did, but I would never ever spend the night in a motel or my apartment with Nathan, honest Ms. Dolly."

Vince couldn't help himself, so he asked, "You would never chase Nathan under the sheets, Sierra?"

"How would I know that, because we've only had one date?"

Desiree asked, "So, Mr. Army Hero asked you out. Where did you go?"

By then, the rest of the office was crowded around Sierra's console, so they could hear the minute by minute description of this romantic interlude. There wasn't anything better than hearing about a hot, sexy date where sweaty flesh was against sweaty flesh in the throngs of animal lust. Oh yes, the more lusting the better.

"Nathan came over to Millie's farmhouse and helped us put up the Christmas tree and all the decorations. When we finished, the farmhouse was gorgeous, and the tree is one of the most beautiful trees I have ever seen. Little Timbo was excited and had the time of his life helping us put lights and ornaments on the tree."

"The ladies grilled hamburgers and hot dogs with all the trimmings, so we could enjoy a meal together and get a piece of Nathan's welcome back home cake."

"He asked me out to a movie and dinner, Sunday. He was so excited about his new car he bought, so he wanted me to ride in it as his first passenger. We took in a movie in Fredericksburg, and we ate dinner at the Globe and Laurel. We ate and talked about all kinds of things. When he took me home, he said this weekend was paradise after coming home from hell. When he said that, I didn't know what to say to him, so I just hugged him and said I understood."

Dolly replied, "You did the right thing. Remember, he's been in combat and has seen the horrors of war. All of us need to love and give him the support he needs."

Shontelle asked, "Did he kiss you good night, girl?"

"Yes he did, and it was a mighty good kiss, too."

Desiree asked, "Did he ask you out, again?"

"We're having dinner Wednesday evening and then shop for Christmas decorations and a tree for his apartment."

Diana chimed in, "You go girl! I thought you said you were Miss Plain Jane and an ugly toad."

"I'm sorry I feel that way, but I don't have much luck with men. I'll probably do something wrong, and he'll dump me like the other men did."

Dolly chimed in, "Maybe, you don't need luck. Don't change, because there isn't anything wrong with you, Sierra. Keep your standards high, because there are a lot of trashy people out there who would just love to drag you down in the gutter with them."

"I never thought that way about it, Ms. Dolly."

Jason jumped in and said, "Sierra, make sure you clean the crap off the sidewalk lover boy's white horse left behind."

She laughed and said, "I'll get right on it, Jason."

Dolly looked around and said, "Okay, kindergarten class it's time to get back to work."

Shontelle stomped back to her desk, threw her hip out to Dolly and said, "I'm transferring to another class. So, take that, missy!"

Everyone had a good laugh, and the three went back to Dolly's office. Vince looked at Dolly and said, "Boss, you don't need me to loosen things up around here, because you're doing just fine on your own."

Desiree piped in, "It's about time you turned over a new

leaf. I think you and Art are chasing each other under the sheets, and married life has made you giddy."

"For crying out loud in a bucket, Desiree, you are the one who's giddy."

Vince joined in and said, "Falling in love sure turned your brain into fluff, Dolly. Next thing you know, you'll be pregnant."

"Sorry to disappoint you, but I'm past the mama stage, Vince."

Desiree shouted, "I knew it! Dolly's going to give birth to a fat ass squirrel that looks just like her!"

The three roared with laughter and emptied a box of Kleenex while they were at it. Finally, Dolly signed all the paperwork Desiree plopped on her desk, so her cousin could get back to her office.

Dolly looked at Vince and said, "I'm very proud of you, because you kept Freestone operating at a high level and handled every emergency to perfection. I know you would rather be investigating, but you are far more valuable to me as Supervisor of Investigative Teams and my personal assistant. I want to be careful with Dan, because I don't want to stress him out. I want you to tell me if you think Dan needs an assistant."

"I will, Dolly."

"You have been in the pressure cooker since I had my

surgery; therefore, I'm giving you a direct order with no argument. I want you to take a week off starting tomorrow. I've already talked to Kris about this, and she agrees with me, totally. Vickie went back to work at RG Accountants, so she and David want Kris and you to have this time together. Vince, I want you to relax, unwind, and recharge your batteries."

"I won't argue with you, because I learned something in the last several months, Dolly. All of us need to get away from our kind of work and relax. We need time to heal emotionally and mentally, or we'll go stark raving crazy."

"If you have one of your sightings or feelings, make sure you let the task force know about it."

"I will, Boss."

"Good! Now, I want to ask you something. Dr. and Mrs. Bronner have two vehicles that are paid for parked at their home. Is there anyone at Freestone who desperately needs a vehicle?"

"What kind of vehicles are they?"

"There is a 2009 Chrysler Town and Country minivan, and a 2007 Cadillac CTS. Both of them have low mileage and are in mint condition."

"Dolly, I know Shontelle needs one, badly. You know what a financial mess her ex-husband put her in. That bucket of bolts she's driving costs her money, constantly."

"I can't think of a better early Christmas present for her than the minivan and some extra bonus money from

Freestone. What do you think?"

"That sounds like a winner to me. Katie Shuler drives an old car around, because she's trying to pay off her student loans from college."

"I didn't know she was strapped like that, so I think she needs a Cadillac CTS and some extra bonus money for Christmas from Freestone. Do you agree?"

"Dolly, whatever you want to do is fine with me. It's great to play Santa Claus when you know a person needs it and will appreciate what you're doing for them."

"Art and I will find out what the blue book price is for each vehicle, and then Art and I will put that money into Timmy's trust."

Dolly asked Vince to update her on each investigative team, so she would know what team would be available to handle a new case.

Vince told her Travis Spangler was back from leave, so he assigned him to Task Force Bronner. Dolly knew Cody McCaslin was on Timmy's security detail, so right now they would stay where they were. Team 8 would start their missing person's case December 3rd.

At the present time, Freestone didn't have a team available to take a new case. If it was necessary, Vince could pull Cody and Travis off their separate assignments to take a case. Dolly was aware that Freestone might have to form a new investigative team if the organization kept growing.

Monday morning, Task Force Bronner was back at Bronner Pharmaceuticals to continue interviewing the staff. Dr. Lim called Detective Gage into his office to let him know Dillon Carr didn't show up for work, and he didn't call in sick which was very unusual for him. His next door neighbor said his truck wasn't parked at his house, and he wasn't at home.

Gage called the Warren County police in Front Royal, gave them the short version of the Bronner Case, and asked them to check Carr's cabin.

Becky stood by Emma's bed to bring her out of her coma.

"Can you hear me, Emma?"

"Yes, and I can see you in the bright light."

"Do you want to be a giver?"

"Yes, and give me another chance to make things right, please."

"Take a deep breath, Emma."

"My head hurts, badly."

"Move your fingers and take another deep breath."

"I want to see my mom and dad, again."

"Open your eyes, because you've been given a second chance, Emma."

"I will never forget you, Becky."

Emma opened her eyes, moved her fingers, and moaned. Her mother jumped out of the chair next to Emma's bed and took her daughter's hand. Emma looked at her mother, smiled, and said, "I love you, and I'm so very glad to see you, Mom."

Her mother called for the nurses and burst into tears. Between sobs she said, "We've been so worried about you and prayed you would come back to us, so we could tell you how much we love you. Baby, whatever it takes to get you back on your feet, we'll do it."

Emma's nurses rushed through the curtains and checked her from head to toe. They asked all kinds of questions and were thrilled she was clear headed. Emma complained about a headache, being thirsty, and hungry. Her nurses promised her they could take care of all three, shortly.

Her mother asked, "Who attacked you like an animal, honey?"

Emma thought for a few seconds and said, "It was Dillon Carr. That lowlife tried to kill me, and I don't know why he would do such a thing."

Freestone's security guard introduced himself and asked her to tell him what happened, so they could arrest Carr before he could flee. He called Detective Gage with the good news, and the information was relayed to Warren County.

When the county deputies got to Carr's cabin and saw his

truck parked, they spread out and searched the area, carefully. When they got to the dry well, one deputy said, "It looks like he took a nose dive into the well."

Another deputy remarked, "Looks like he won't be attacking anymore women, and you'd think the dumb prick would have stayed away from the rotten boards. Well, I guess we better get his sorry hide out of this dry well."

Dillon Carr's body was recovered, and the county coroner transported the body to be autopsied. Warren County said they would contact Task Force Bronner with the results as soon as possible. In their opinion, it appeared to be an accident.

Gage requested a DNA sample, Carr's truck, cell phone, and his laptop be sent to Freestone. Also, he asked the coroner to look for fingernail scratches consistent with Emma's attack.

The task force headed back to Freestone to discuss Dillon Carr before they had to be at the Bronner's church for the memorial service. Detective Gage called Dolly and Vince to let them know about Emma and Carr.

Dolly looked at Vince and asked, "Do you think Carr is the murderer?"

"I think he did the dirty work, but someone else told him to do it, in my opinion. Of course, I'm sure he got paid to do the work."

"What do you base that opinion on?"

"The E and B I saw fits right in the middle of Emily Bronner and Emma Baker. My gut tells me Emily was a mistake, and the kingpin wanted Emma dead, instead."

"I tend to agree with you. Do you think this kingpin will go after Emma, again?"

"Dolly, if the kingpin wants Emma dead badly enough, then the woman is still in danger."

"I'm going to continue our security detail at the hospital and at her home unless she says no, because we can't force the detail on her."

"We'll have to explain our theory, so she'll know she's still in danger."

"Let's put the story out that Emma has come out of her coma, but she doesn't remember the attack. That might buy us more time to catch this lunatic. I'll call Gage and tell him to put that story out."

When the task force got back to Freestone, they met in their conference room to go over today's events and the memorial service.

Gage asked, "Do you think we have the killer?"

Ryan answered, "He's the killer, but I think there's another person involved. Carr taking a nose dive in the dry well wasn't an accident, in my opinion. I think someone pushed him, because he didn't kill Emma."

Hansen stated, "We need to get a search warrant for his

house, and get permission to search his cabin from Warren County. There has to be something in either place that might lead us to the person who ordered the hit. Let's call this person Viper for the time being. Vince insists a second person is calling the shots, and if that's the case, the killing is not over."

Before 7:00 pm the church was completely full with people standing where they could find a place. What tore Byron's heart out was seeing so many of Greta and Timmy's classmates there sobbing in their parent's arms.

The minister talked about Dr. Bronner's quiet gentle manner, and all the projects he funded from the shadows away from the limelight. Fondly, he talked about Greta and Timmy playing the piano when the youth choir sang. Also, the minister talked about the volunteer work Emily Bronner did at the food bank and soup kitchen. While the minister honored the memory of the Bronner family, he prayed Timmy would be found alive and safe.

While he spoke, the task force scanned the mourners looking for anything unusual or out of place. There were lots of people crying or dabbing tears, and there were the stoic ones who had expressionless faces as if they were staring off in space. What surprised the task force the most was all the stuffed animals, cards, letters, and flowers that were placed on the floor below the pulpit. What was going to happen to all these things?

When the eloquent memorial service was over, the minister was bombarded with questions about Timmy, and what they could do to help. The agents milled around the crowd hoping to pick up useful information.

At this point, the task force's story was working, because the people associated with the company believed Emma was awake, but couldn't remember the attack. They believed Dillon Carr fell into his dry well while he was replacing rotten boards, accidently. Hopefully, this would give the task force more time to narrow the field of suspects.

Detective Gage asked the minister if he could pack up the stuffed animals, cards, and letters left at the pulpit, so he could take them to Freestone. Gage wanted to make sure there were no nasty surprises left, and he didn't want anyone to know these items would be saved for Timmy in the future.

The minister thanked Gage for leaving the flowers, because they could be given to the church's elderly who were receiving meals on wheels from the church.

When Task Force Bronner left the church for home, each member was touched by the service, deeply. They had to find the evil person who ordered these hits before someone else was murdered.

"Dillon, the only thing you did right was killing Newby. You screwed up twice, you stupid prick! Did you think I was going to pay you big bucks for two screw ups? Even though Emma can't remember the attack, I

have to decide whether I want her dead. Also, I have some more people to remove from the game, so do I hire another jerk to do it, or do I handle it myself?"

CHAPTER 11

Monday, Timmy was introduced to his new tutor, Deanna Perry. They seemed to hit it off right away, so they set up their school room in Millie's living room where they could have some privacy.

Thanks to Jason in cyber security, Art was able to give Miss Perry copies of Timmy's records and curriculum plan from Stargate Academy. Timmy let her know he wanted to learn sign language and how to speak Spanish, shortly.

The two got down to business as they planned each day's schedule to include time for his music. She brought a lot of sheet music to leave with him to practice with. While talking with him, Miss Perry learned about the fun he had line dancing, so they decided to include that as a sort of recess along with the Greedy Gut feeding frenzy which blew her away.

The tutor let the 3M ladies know what Timmy needed as far as supplies, so they could get those things for him by tomorrow. Unfortunately, Timmy's laptop was stolen when his family was killed, so that became number one on the list.

Adam and Mandy left with the tutor's list and headed to Manassas to buy those items. They had to get Mandy her engagement ring, look at furniture, and order wedding invitations. They ate dinner at a nice restaurant to celebrate their engagement. The couple had a lot to do before the wedding, so they could get the stone farmhouse ready for them and Timmy.

They already decided to set up one of the eight bedrooms as Timmy's school room/office, his bedroom, and a master bedroom for them. Two bedroom suites from Dr. Bronner's house were already set up. Mandy and Adam bought furniture for the living room, their bedroom, and the family room. Dolly told them Freestone would furnish a bedroom and office, set up the kitchen, and stock the house with groceries.

When they got back from dinner, everyone loved her engagement ring, and the wedding band she bought for Adam. Even Timbo got caught up in the excitement when he was told he would be the ring bearer.

The couple didn't forget Timmy's birthday was Saturday, so they got him some presents they hoped he would love and cherish. Mabel was baking him a big cake to feed all the people who were invited to his party. Everybody hoped Timbo wouldn't be too sad, because he had a brand new bunch of relatives to look after him.

Mandy and Adam put all his school supplies in the living room, and Adam set up his laptop for school the next day. Timbo seemed to be happy about his tutor and eager to get back into a routine. Apparently, Miss Perry was more advanced on the piano than his teacher at the Academy, so he was excited to be challenged once again.

The ladies told Mandy and Adam the boy did his homework and practiced on the piano. Mandy had to laugh when she brought Timbo down after his bath, because he was fast asleep in Adam's arms in about five minutes. Obviously, Timbo had a very busy day back in school.

Tomorrow, Millie and Mandy were going into Manassas to look at wedding dresses at a bridal shop Millie knew about. In her opinion, this lady had a large selection at very reasonable prices. After that they were going to order flowers for the farmhouse.

Mabel and Adam were going to his apartment to pack up his clothes and everything the two could get in his truck and Mabel's car. Sunday, some agents he knew were going to help him move some furniture to the stone farmhouse. Adam told the guys they were welcome to anything that wasn't moved. He knew the guys would jump on the other stuff, because they were bachelors who could use whatever was given to them.

By Wednesday, Heather had Carr's cell phone, briefcase, laptop, and truck. She was able to confirm Carr's truck caused the damage to Dr. Newby's car when he forced the car off the road. When Heather was going over Carr's cellphone, she came across a text message she knew the task force would want to know about. She charged into the conference room and shouted, "Gage, you have to see this!"

"Okay, settle down before you have a hissy fit, Heather."

"Carr received a text message two days before Thanksgiving at 6:11 pm saying, the wrong E. B., you idiot! Get it right! He texted back, I'll take care of it."

Gage jumped up and shouted, "Hot Dang! Carr was the hit man for someone else, and it looks like Emily Bronner was murdered by mistake!"

Hansen added, "Emma Baker was attacked around 7:30 pm, so that gave Carr time to drive to her house from his."

Heather said, "I'm sorry I got so excited, but I knew this was big. I'll look for more messages like this one, and I'll find out what cell tower it originated from. At least, that will narrow the area you have to search."

Brad remarked, "Let the hounds loose, we have a scent!"

Byron stated, "Carr's financial report doesn't show any red flags, and I feel he was paid for the hits. Let's have Jason look for an offshore account he might have put money into. The man might have had plans to slip out of the country and live like a king on one of the islands."

Heather went back to her lab, and one of her assistants called her attention to a folded item larger than a wallet. When she opened it, it contained a U. S. Passport and a Virginia's driver's license with Carr's picture, but the name was John D. Meadows. She picked up another evidence bag with brochures from Aruba and Mexico. She charged back into the conference room and showed Gage the evidence bags.

Gage shouted, "Holy crap! That low life was headed out of the country. Heather, take some deep breaths, so you can calm down. Girl, you did great, and we know you are the best. I'll have Jason check John Meadows out."

It wasn't long before Jason got a hit on an account in the name of John D. Meadows or Taylor W. Meadows with a balance of $872,421.12. Jason said, "I would have found him anyway, because Carr's middle name is John, and he lives on

Green Meadow Road. How stupid was that name choice? The second name is going to take longer, because Taylor can be male or female. How much you want to bet Taylor W. Meadows is right in the middle of all this mess?"

Hansen added, "Let's put Taylor on the watch list. Maybe, we'll get lucky and stop our suspect from leaving the country."

Ryan asked, "Could our financial officer be stealing money from the company a little at the time over the years?"

Gage replied, "Yep, and our audit should be able to find how much and how he did it."

Jason asked, "Do you want me to play with the balance in this account, Boss?"

Gage answered, "If you can do that without alarming the world we did this, you work your magic, Jason."

"Don't worry, Boss."

That evening, Hansen went to see Emma Baker, because he wanted to ask her some questions and explain to her she was still in danger. When he walked in, he could tell she was doing a lot better, and her parents were much more relaxed.

Hansen told them what they knew about Dillon Carr, and their story about her not remembering the attack was working, so far. She understood the danger she was still in, so her parents agreed Emma needed protection. Hansen told them about Freestone, and her parents insisted they meet Director Hamilton and arrange protection for Emma when she was discharged from the hospital.

Hansen asked, "Emma, how well did you know Carr?"

"We went out a couple of times, but nothing impressed me, so I moved on."

Hansen asked, "Who else did you date in the company?"

"I had a fling with Dr. Newby that didn't last long, so I moved on. I dated Harry Dent a few times, but that didn't last, because he was all hands and no class. In other words, he was a horny rabbit in bunny heaven. I've dated Dr. Tanner a few times, but all he talked about was his very expensive divorce."

"Can you think of anyone who would want to kill you by using Carr as a hit man?"

"I have no idea, because I've never had an argument with any of my co-workers. I didn't steal anybody's boyfriend, and I can't imagine Harry Dent wanting me dead."

Hansen added, "Dillon Carr was willing to kill you for money."

"Oh Lord, I didn't think about that angle."

Hansen continued, "Freestone is going to continue your security detail in the hospital. Mrs. Baker, the three of you decide what you want to do when Emma is discharged from the hospital after you've met with Dolly Hamilton."

Mrs. Baker asked, "What would you do, detective?"

"I'd have Freestone put you in one of their safe houses where it's secure. You don't want anyone to know where you are, Emma."

Mr. Baker replied, "We want Emma safe from this maniac. Honey, we're going to do this to keep our baby safe."

Thursday morning, Viper took a pass key, opened an office door, pulled out the bottom drawer to the desk, and removed a .22 pistol. Viper left with the weapon and went back to work. Several people knew why the pistol was there, but they would never guess what the owner was going to do with it next.

That evening around 7:00 pm, Viper waited for the next victim to come home from the gym. The victim pulled into the garage, closed the garage door, and put his key in the door that led into the kitchen. Quietly, Viper slipped behind him, aimed the pistol at his head, and pulled the trigger. The victim collapsed near the door as his blood formed a pool around his head. Viper slipped through the kitchen and out the sliding glass doors. While driving home, Viper thought, *"I got even with you; what a shame! At least, I know you are dead, because I hate screw ups like Dillon Carr. I'm almost ready to claim my golden egg."*

Friday morning, Viper slipped back into the office, put the pistol back in the bottom drawer of the desk, and went back to work.

A scientist in the Production Division looked at a colleague and asked, "Why hasn't Dr. Tanner shown up for work? He hasn't called in sick, so this just isn't like him. I got a bad feeling about this, especially with people being killed or attacked in this company. The place is starting to give me the creeps."

"I don't live too far from him, so I'll call my wife and have her check his house."

The wife knocked on Dr. Tanner's front door, but nobody answered. She went around back and looked through the sliding glass doors, but there was no Tanner. When she walked around the garage, she looked through the window and saw him lying face down with his legs still on the steps to the door. The wife called her husband and 911. She hoped Tanner didn't have a heart attack or a stroke.

When the police and ambulance arrived, she showed them the window in the garage and told them she didn't try any of the doors. The police discovered the sliding glass doors were unlocked, so they entered the house and walked towards the victim only to find Tanner dead from a gunshot wound to the head. They secured the area and called Sheriff Patterson with the news. The Sheriff sent the techs and the medical examiner to the address and called Detective Hansen.

The task force was going over interviews and printouts when Hansen got the call. When he hung up, he looked at the team and explained what had happened.

Gage remarked, "Viper is at it, again. I wonder if Viper did the dirty work or hired a hit man."

Ryan asked, "Didn't Tanner have a nasty argument with Dr. Zocrist?"

Brad answered, "That's right, and Zocrist goes to the shooting range every Tuesday and Wednesday right after work. Maybe, he paid Tanner a little visit?"

Hansen told Gage, "We need to get to Zocrist right away. The rest of you stay here and pour over all these printouts while Gage and I pay Zocrist a visit."

Hansen called the deputies at the crime scene to make sure the wife didn't call her husband with the news that Tanner was shot. The deputy assured him she didn't know what happened to him, and she was sitting in his cruiser. Hansen called for backup to meet him at Bronner Pharmaceuticals, so they could go in together to question Zocrist.

The two detectives walked into the man's office while two deputies stood outside.

Hansen asked, "Dr. Zocrist, when was the last time you saw Dr. Tanner?"

"I saw him yesterday afternoon in the Production Division."

"Did you have an argument with him yesterday?"

"No, I just saw him at a distance."

Hansen continued, "I understand you keep a pistol in your office, because you go to a shooting range twice a week and carry drugs, at times."

"Yes, I keep it in my desk, and when I'm not in my office I keep the door locked. What's going on here, Detective Hansen?"

"Take the pistol out of the desk drawer very slowly, put it on the desk top, and step away from the desk."

Zocrist did what he was told, and Hansen put gloves on and picked up the .22 handgun to examine it. He looked at the doctor and said, "This weapon has been fired, recently."

Zocrist shouted, "That's impossible, because I always clean my gun after I go to the range!"

Gage asked, "Where were you last night around 7:00 pm?"

"I was having dinner with Maria Santana at a restaurant in Manassas."

"How long were you there?"

"We got there around 6:00 pm and left around 8:00 pm. I know the manager very well, so he can vouch for me, and I used a credit card to pay for the meal."

"Does anyone else have a key to your office?"

"No one has a key to my office. I demand to know what

this is all about!"

"Dr. Tanner was found shot to death in his home last night."

"Listen, I didn't like the prick, but I didn't kill him! Maybe, he shot himself, because he was having a lot of money problems."

"Did you hire someone else to do the dirty work?"

"I certainly did not! I'm not saying another word until I call my lawyer!"

"That's fine, doctor. Have him meet you at the police station, so we can iron things out. We'll need to check out your alibi."

The wild fire of gossip pleased Viper. *"Poor Dr. Tanner was shot to death, and Dr. Zocrist is a suspect at the police station. It will take you a while to wiggle out of this mess. Have a nice day, Colin."*

Hansen sent Gage back to Freestone with the evidence bag containing Dr. Zocrist's .22 pistol, so he could take Zocrist to the station. He knew the techs found the bullet, and all the evidence was headed to Freestone. The medical examiner was going to perform the autopsy in Heather's suite. If that was the murder weapon and Zocrist's alibi checked out, this became a different can of worms.

Hansen thought, "Did Zocrist hire someone to do it? Did someone else have a key to his office door and stole the gun? Security would have a master key, so did one of them steal the gun?

The security tapes were headed to Freestone, so the task force could look through them for any clues. Hansen wanted to have a serious talk with Harry Dent, because he might be involved in this mess.

Friday evening, Detective Hansen was able to verify Dr. Zocrist's alibi, and Heather verified the .22 pistol was the murder weapon. Dr. Zocrist didn't pull the trigger, but did he hire someone to do it? He was right; this was a different can of worms. He hoped the security tapes would help him get some answers. He didn't have any other choice, so Dr. Zocrist was released and told to stay available in case they needed to ask him some more questions.

CHAPTER 12

Saturday, Timmy was treated to a special birthday party attended by a whole boat load of new crazy relatives. Mabel baked a beautiful red velvet cake for him and all the guests to eat.

Dolly and Art gave him the Rosetta stone for Spanish, so he could practice any time he wanted.

Sierra and Sheridan gave him some DVDs he asked for.

Dan and Erika gave him some country CDs he really liked.

Millie and Mabel found out Timbo loved to put models together, so they bought him several to put together.

Gil gave him a Christmas sweatshirt and holiday socks.

Adam and Mandy found out Timbo loved Panda bears, so they bought him a snow globe music box with Pandas inside, a shirt with a Panda on it, and a little boy cowboy hat and boots he could wear line dancing. He squealed and jumped up and down every time he opened up a present, but when he opened up the hat and boots Timbo launched himself around Mandy and cried.

Between sobs he said, "I love my new hat and boots, because they are very special."

Adam replied, "Now, when your daddy, mommy, and sissy watch you dance, you will be dancing in style like Mabel."

Everyone had to swallow knots in their throats when they

saw his tears of happiness; however, Adam's tickling got Timmy laughing, again.

The group decided to put on some music, so Timbo could wear his new hat and boots. He grabbed Mabel's hand and told her to dance with him. Then, he told Art and Dolly to watch, so they could dance, later. Again, Timbo, Mabel, Gil, and Millie fell right in sync with each other.

Art watched for a while and decided this had to be fun. He grabbed Dolly's hand and joined the group. In no time flat, both picked up Timbo's lead and were dancing like pros.

Dolly commented, "This is a lot of fun, Cricket! You sure do know how to move and groove, sweetie."

Art replied, "I was going to say the same thing about you. No wonder Walt loves to do this. We need to get some music like this, so we can line dance at home."

Dolly looked at Art and said, "We'd start line dancing, and the line would end up in the bedroom, Arthur Hamilton."

"What can I say? Both are excellent forms of exercise, Dolly Hamilton."

Mabel looked at both of them and asked, "What are you going to do; line dance all over the mattress or under the sheets, Art?"

Dolly answered, "He'll line dance under the sheets, and we'll end up all twisted up like worms on a fishing hook."

Mabel shot back, "I hope Art doesn't end up with the hook caught in his behind."

Millie chimed in, "Mabel, remember whose listening to this exchange, sister dear."

Mabel fired back, "Loosen up your girdle! He doesn't know what we're talking about, sister dear."

Timbo put his hands on his hips and said, "You can't line dance on a bed, because it's too bouncy, sister dear."

Mabel told Timbo, "You're absolutely right, Timbo. Art and Dolly should line dance in the shower and forget the bed."

Timbo looked puzzled and said, "You can't line dance in the shower, because it's not big enough and you'd get wet, Aunt Mabel."

Millie was just about ready to wring Mabel's neck like a chicken, but she controlled herself. Everyone else was laughing like hyenas on catnip. Leave it to Mabel to blow in like a tornado to stir up that bucket of poop.

Before the birthday guests said their goodbyes, Timbo played the piano for them. Of course, that led to lots of hugs and kisses.

Mabel got extra hugs and kisses, because she was flying out Sunday to spend a few days with her daughter's family in Wisconsin. Adam was taking her to the airport to catch her flight out of Dulles.

Sunday, Dolly and Art went out to the Bronner home to move the last items to the stone farmhouse.

Walt and Mitch looked around to see what Mitch would need once he bought the property. He accepted the realtor's price and was ready to get the ball rolling. The house would be perfect for agents to stay in until the stone farmhouse apartments were ready to move into. What items Mitch had in storage could be delivered any time. That didn't leave a whole lot left to buy.

Dolly brought extra help along, so they could drive Bronner's two vehicles back to Freestone to surprise two wonderful members of the Freestone family.

Sunday, Nathan and Sierra decorated his apartment for Christmas and put up his Christmas tree. When the decorating was finished, Sierra noticed tears rolling down Nathan's cheeks. She hugged him close and said the apartment looked so beautiful even she had tears in her eyes. He kissed her and thanked her for understanding what he was going through. They went to dinner and picked up some decorations for her apartment. Tuesday, he was coming over to help her decorate her apartment, put her tree up, and pig out on pizza.

Sierra thought to herself come Monday morning those nutty co-workers at Freestone were probably going to grill her good about their date. She smiled when she thought about Shontelle. One of these days, someone was going to cross her path and knock her for a loop. When that happened, she was going to have fun teasing Shontelle right out of her britches.

When Hansen talked to Harry Dent, he had a solid alibi for the night Dr. Tanner was murdered. Hansen was really angry when he found out the camera in the hallway where all the scientist's offices were located wasn't working. Dent showed him the work order request sent to maintenance to repair or replace the camera. When maintenance was contacted, they said they hadn't gotten around to that work order, yet. Sometimes, Hansen felt like he was being flushed down a toilet.

Jesse Rice met with Hansen and told him what he saw at work. He agreed to wear a wire when he confronted Viper.

Monday, Viper got out of the car when Jesse walked over to the vehicle.

Viper asked, *"What are you doing here?"*

"I saw you go into Dr. Zocrist's office Thursday and Friday. You took his .22 pistol and then returned it Friday morning."

Viper replied, *"I did no such thing! Get out of here!"*

"What did you do with half of Dillon Carr's money in his offshore account in Aruba?"

Viper shot back, *"I haven't done a thing with it. Besides, part of that money is mine. What did you do with the money?"*

"Wait a minute! Dillon and I were going to Aruba, split the money, and live in the lap of luxury."

Viper fired back, *"Dillon and I were going to Aruba and do the same thing."*

"You mean Dillon was going to double cross me and leave the country with you."

"That lowlife was taking you and leaving me behind."

"Maybe, Dillon planned to double cross both of us."

"Then, why is half of the money missing?"

"Listen, I don't like talking about this problem here. Let's meet at the Gaslight Restaurant around 6:00 pm, because they have some areas where we can talk, privately. Don't try to pull anything stupid, or I'll sing like a canary."

"I'll be there at 6:00 pm, and you make sure you don't do anything stupid, either."

Detective Hansen listened to the conversation from the wire and just shook his head. "Well Jason, your magic just put a person in a tailspin. Viper thinks they've been double crossed by Dillon Carr. I love it! Alright, let's put our two agents in the restaurant and set up everything with the manager. Let's listen in on their conversation to see if anyone else is involved, because this should be a hum dinger."

Gage looked up and remarked, "How many people are trying to kill each other in this weird company?"

Ryan answered, "We know Carr killed Dr. Newby, the Bronner family, and tried to kill Emma. Did Viper hire Dillon to do it?"

Brad remarked, "If we don't watch it, Viper is going to kill Jesse."

Byron added, "Viper is going to chase around trying to find the money. Viper is going to think someone in the company took the money or moved it to another account. What Viper doesn't know is our whiz kid moved the money. I just love this circus."

Hansen commented, "We're not going to move until we know how big this circus is. By the way, Jesse is doing a great job for us."

Monday morning, Shontelle stomped into work mad as a hornet. "Does anybody have a bazooka I can borrow?"

Jason asked, "What on earth do you want a bazooka for?"

Shontelle answered, "My bucket of rusted bolts just died on me. I'm going to blow it's rusted behind all the way to the nearest junkyard. It's going to cost me $2,200.00 to fix it, so why are the car gods dumping on me?"

Dolly smiled and walked out to the work station area.

"Shontelle, I want you in my office right away, young lady!"

Shontelle stomped into Dolly's office like a southern belle whirlwind and said, "Ms. Dolly, I'm in no mood to be kicked to the curb, today. I'm already floating upside down in the sewer and drowning in shit."

Dolly warned, "Shontelle, behave yourself, because we have business to take care of."

Shontelle asked, "What businesses are you talking about, because I'm pissed right now and in no mood for games, missy?"

Dolly said, "Sign these papers, clean out your dead car, take the plates off it, and take these keys."

"Ms. Dolly, I'm in no mood to tiptoe through the dead tulips and shaft thy neighbor kind of shit."

Dolly got up, pulled Shontelle into the work area, dragged her outside, and marched her over to her early Christmas present. "Now, shut your flapping jaws, take these keys, and open up your almost new van, Shontelle."

"Wha, wha, what's going on, Ms. Dolly? Have you gone crazy?"

"Sweet Jesus, don't you understand English, girl? Freestone is giving you this van, because you need it."

Shontelle jumped up and down, burst into tears, and hugged Dolly. When she was about half way composed, she opened the door, and slid in the front seat.

"This is the most beautiful van I have ever seen. Ms. Dolly,

I've never received a gift like this in my entire life. I don't know how I can ever repay you."

Dolly remarked, "You have repaid me by being you, already. Don't change, because there's nothing wrong with you, Shontelle. Now, where is your dead car?"

"It died across the street at the gas station."

"Okay, I'll have Jason help you clean it out and get the tags. You take the rest of the day off, so you can go to the DMV. Don't forget to check the van's glove compartment, because there's an envelope in it for you. I'll have Jason call to get your bucket of bolts towed to the nearest junkyard."

"Ms. Dolly, I'm a pile of excited nerves, right now. I'll never let you down, and you can count on me whenever you need me."

"Go inside, get your purse, and freshen up your makeup in the bathroom. You have a lot to do."

Shontelle made a beeline to get her purse and headed straight for the bathroom, because she was about to pee in her britches. She was shaking so badly, she hoped she wouldn't be too late.

When Dolly walked back inside, she told Sierra to call Katie Shuler, and tell her to be in her office at 9:30 am, tomorrow.

Sierra asked, "Is there something wrong, Ms. Dolly?"

"No, everything is fine and dandy."

Sierra asked, "Is Shontelle, alright?"

"Honey, she is more than alright. Jason, when Shontelle gets out of the bathroom, she'll need you to help her do a few things outside."

Monday evening around 6:00 pm two Freestone agents were sitting in the restaurant eating their salads when the two walked inside. The manager seated them at a secluded table, gave them menus, and took their drink orders.

One agent said, "Okay folks, the show is about to begin."

Before they got down to business, the mole and Viper got their drinks and ordered their meals.

"Why did you say part of Dillon's money was yours?"

Viper replied, *"I paid him to take care of Dr. Newby. At least, he did that right."*

"You mean he was supposed to take care of more?"

"Yes, but he screwed both of them up. Of course, I didn't pay him for those screw ups."

"Dillon was a lot of mouth and promises he didn't keep."

"Yes, and I found that out the hard way."

"Did Dillon get you a phony passport and driver's license?"

"Yes, my fake name is Taylor W. Meadows."

"That low life prick! My passport and license are in the

same name."

"He told me we would fly out on a private jet to Aruba."

"He told me the same thing. There's no way we could have gotten into Aruba with two passports in the same name."

"That prick was going to fly to Aruba alone or with someone else."

"That means someone else has the same passport and license as we have. They must be in Aruba spending that money, right now."

"Dillon could have taken half of the money and moved it into another account just for him. That prick knew we wouldn't be able to get into the country with these passports.

"He was playing us like fools."

"Do you believe he fell into that dry well, accidently?"

"If he didn't, then we have a big problem."

"You didn't push him in?"

"Shit no, I thought you probably did."

"I have no idea where his cabin is."

"I never knew he had a cabin."

"I think someone pushed him into that well."

"Then, who killed Dillon?"

"Darn, this mess is making my head spin. If we find out who killed him, we'll find the money."

"I hired Dillon to take care of someone, but he screwed that up, and I lost my money."

"What happened?"

"I told him to take care of Dr. Tanner, but Dillon was dead when Tanner was killed."

"Why did you want Tanner removed?"

"The lowlife owed me money I never got back!"

"You can thank me for that job. I took care of Tanner myself."

"Shit, I should have hired you. What did he do to you?"

"Let's say I had a score to settle with him."

"How are we going to find Dillon's killer?"

"I don't know. Maybe, it's one of his former or present girlfriends."

"That's a good place to start."

"Let's eat dinner, go home, and think about our next moves. Do you want to meet here at six, tomorrow night?"

"That sounds good to me."

The task force met to discuss the secret rendezvous at the restaurant, Tuesday morning.

Hansen spoke up, "Well team, I'd say we have a real circus on our hands. Now, we know Viper killed Dr. Tanner and hired Carr to kill Newby and Emma. We have Carr screwing up and killing the Bronner family by mistake. Viper doesn't know who killed Carr."

Gage remarked, "So, Viper thinks Carr's killer has the money. I love this rollercoaster."

Ryan asked, "Do we arrest Viper tonight at the restaurant?"

Hansen answered, "No, I want them to lead me to Carr's killer. Viper has accepted Jesse Rice as part of Carr's con, so he can keep wearing our wire. We'll be right there when the time is right to make the arrest."

Brad commented, "Thank heavens, he came to us with his suspicions and told us what he saw. Jesse is doing a great job."

Hansen continued, "Tonight, two different Freestone

agents will be in the restaurant, and I'm anxious to see what Viper wants to do."

Byron added, "I hope this trap works, because I think this gives us our best chance to smoke out the killer."

CHAPTER 13

Agent Katie Shuler knocked on Dolly's office door at 9:30 am.

"Come on in and sit right here in this chair."

Katie asked, "Your request seemed serious, so have I done something wrong, Ms. Dolly?"

"You are a fine agent, but I need to ask you some questions."

"Ask all the questions you want, Boss."

"What kind of shape is your car in?"

"Ms. Dolly, I know agents have to have a dependable vehicle to do our job, but I keep fixing mine, because I don't have the money to buy another one."

"Why can't you buy another one?"

"I'm so sorry, but I'm trying to pay off my student loans and help my parents, too."

"You mean you give your parents money, too?"

"Yes. I buy some of their medications they can't afford."

"Why didn't you come to me with this problem?"

"I was afraid you'd fire me."

"Do I make you feel like I'm a heartless witch?"

"Oh no, I just didn't know what to do. No one wants to admit they're struggling."

"Sign this paperwork and then we're taking a walk."

Poor Katie was on the verge of tears as Dolly led her through the parking lot and stopped in front of a beautiful burgundy Cadillac CTS.

Dolly grabbed her hand and put the car's keys in it. "Now, open up your 2007 Cadillac in mint condition."

Katie burst into tears and hugged Dolly silly. "I don't believe this is happening to me! Oh Ms. Dolly, it's so beautiful! I don't know how I can ever repay you."

"You already have by being a fine agent. Now, take the rest of the day off, so you can go to the DMV. Also, there's an envelope in the glove compartment for you. Tomorrow, I want a list of the medicines you're paying for on my desk."

"Why do you want that?"

"It's none of your business, Katie."

When Dolly got back in her office, Shontelle stormed into the office and said, "Do you realize how much money was in that envelope? There was more than enough to pay off the bills my chicken shit ex-husband of mine ran up."

"I know how much was in the envelope, because I put it there. Now, scoot! I have some work to do."

"You're one fine woman, Ms. Dolly. That was a wonderful

thing you did for me and Katie. You'll always be my Christmas angel."

"Shontelle, get out of my office before we both start bawling. Now, scoot!"

Shontelle stomped to the door, looked over her shoulder and said, "Up yours, missy!"

Both women laughed until their sides hurt. Thank heavens for Kleenex.

Vince and Kris had a wonderful week's vacation in Pigeon Forge. He really needed that time to relax and recharge his batteries, so to speak. In the morning, he got caught up concerning his investigative teams. He was so pleased to hear Team 3 came to a successful ending to their case. They were able to find Amber Ellis alive and living with a relative. Now, the team could go on leave time. Of course, the office was a beehive, because Shontelle and Katie from Team 3 were given mint condition cars.

He checked in with Task Force Bronner to see if they made any progress in the case. When they told him what was going on, he was anxious to know what Viper had to say at tonight's dinner with Jesse.

After lunch Vince stopped by Dolly's office to check in.

"Wow Hollywood, you sure do look a lot better and relaxed. Tell me about your visit to the Inn at Christmas Place."

"You were right, because both of us loved staying at the Christmas Inn, and Kris went crazy at the store across the street. I thought we had enough Christmas decorations, but my lovely wife bought a whole lot more. The shows we went to were great! We'll have to rent an eighteen wheeler to bring back all the stuff, if we go back again."

"Well Vince, Art and I plan to go back there to get more decorations for Freestone next year. We just didn't have enough room last time."

Vince laughed and said, "You better rent an eighteen wheeler, too."

"Vince, you'll be glad to know Shontelle has her van, Katie has her Cadillac, and both got enough money to pay off their bills.

"How did you feel when you gave them their keys?"

"I felt like Santa Claus on an adrenaline rush. It's one of the greatest feelings a person can have. When Art gave Lydia and Kris their classic cars, he taught me what that feeling meant."

"I hope you realize how very special your husband is."

"I certainly do, because I consider myself very blessed to be his wife, Vince."

She asked, "Are you ready for Shiloh and Darren's wedding on Saturday?"

"Yep, Kris got them a beautiful arrangement for a dining room table and several Christmas ornaments."

"I'm really happy Shiloh found a decent man who truly loves her."

"What's the latest on the Timmy front, Dolly?"

"He had a wonderful birthday party, he loves his new tutor, and he's gotten Mabel, Millie, Gil, and us to line dance."

"Holy smoke, that's the last thing I expected to hear. That is fantastic!"

"Mitch Raven is buying the Bronner home, and we can house agents there until the apartments are completed at the stone farmhouse."

"I'm glad to hear that. Well, I have to do some work, so I'll talk to you, later."

Vince left, got a fresh cup of coffee, and sat down at his desk to do some paperwork. He looked up and saw Becky smiling at him.

"There's my little cousin. I'm glad to see you."

"My daddy is coming for me, but another little girl will take my place and help you. Trust her like you trusted me."

"I'm so glad you found your daddy, and the peace you were looking for. I hope one day we'll see each other, again. Thank you for everything you did for me and the others."

Becky faded away along with her cat, Patches. Suddenly, Vince felt sad and uncertain about his gift. Even though he would miss her, he just had to trust what Becky told him.

Tuesday evening, the two Freestone agents were in the restaurant eating when Viper and Jesse walked in. The manager put them at another secluded table, and took their meal and drink orders.

Viper said, *"I've been thinking about this problem, and I think we should pay a visit to Dillon's girlfriends, especially the ones he dated the most. Lord knows, the man was a dating machine."*

"I agree, because one of them has that money."

"We don't ask them if they killed Dillon for obvious reasons. We ask them if they were a victim of Dillon's con game."

"You're right, because we don't want to spook the killer."

"Maybe, they'll act funny or slip up and say something that will alert us."

"Dillon dated Hansa, Maria Santana, and Karen Newby several times as well as a waitress at Billy's Bar and Grill, and a woman at the local gym several times. We should start with one of them."

"I think Maria Santana has dated just about every man in the company."

"Oh yea, she's one hot babe, and she has Dr. Zocrist

wrapped around her little finger."

"Okay, let's start with Maria. When I get home, I'll call her to set up a meeting between us."

"What if she's out on a date?"

"Then, I'll call the others until I can set something up. I'll call you when I know something."

"I bet you he pulled his con game on all five."

"Oh yes, Dillon had the golden tongue."

"Did you raise hell with Dillon when he killed the Bronner family?"

"You bet I did! Even though Bronner wasn't much of a leader, he was alright."

"He shouldn't have killed the whole family."

"I texted that idiot to get rid of E B, but he killed the wrong one."

"I hope they find the little boy."

"I asked that prick what he did with the boy, and he told me he threw him into a well."

"Holy shit! You mean the same well he fell into?"

"How would I know?"

"The police didn't say anything about a boy being found in the well."

"Evidently, Dillon lied about that, too. No telling where the boy is. Besides, we have more important things to worry about. Let's eat and get out of here, so I can make some phone calls. Remember, don't pull anything stupid."

"The same thing applies to you, or I'll sing that canary song."

"Listen, we want the money, so we can get out of the country."

"We'll have to use our own passports."

"That's fine, but we need to find that money fast and get to Aruba."

Viper and Jesse left the restaurant and went their separate ways. Jesse prayed Viper would keep him in the hunt.

Around 9:30 pm Viper called Jesse to let him know they were going to Maria's house Thursday evening around 8:00 pm. Hansa said they could come by Friday evening around 7:00 pm, but Mrs. Newby wasn't at home."

Thursday evening, Maria answered the door and let Viper and Jesse in. "You said this meeting was very important, so what's going on?"

Viper asked, *"Did Dillon Carr ever say anything to you about going to Aruba with him?"*

"That low life told me about it, but he was going to take me to Mexico."

Viper asked, *"Was he going to take you there, so you could split a large sum of money and live the easy life?"*

Maria laughed and said, "Dillon was the biggest liar and loser I have ever run across. Listen, I dated him a few times, but I knew he was a con artist, and I certainly didn't want to live in Mexico."

Jesse asked, "Did he give you a fake passport to go with him?"

She laughed and answered, "No, because I told him to buzz off and lie to somebody else."

Jesse asked, "Did you know he had a cabin in the mountains?"

"Dillon wasn't smart enough to own a cabin, so it must belong to someone else. Then, the dumb shit falls in a well. That was priceless! Believe me, I won't miss him."

Viper asked, *"Do you know of anyone else he might have pulled this con on?"*

She commented, "Well, Hansa and Mrs. Newby dated him for a while. Don't tell me you two fell for that line of bullshit?"

Jesse said, "I'm afraid we did."

Maria said, "If Hansa and Mrs. Newby don't work out try most of the women in the cafeteria and the pregnant girl in the IT Department. The man was a dating maniac. Lord knows, what he promised them."

Viper and Jesse pulled into a fast food place and got some coffee.

Viper asked, *"Do you think Maria killed him and has the money?"*

"I don't think so. She was so calm about everything."

"She didn't seem to be worried about our questions or threatened by us."

"She's not high on my guilty list, so far."

"Okay, tomorrow night we'll meet with Hansa and see what she has to say. Maybe, I'll have a meeting set up with Karen Newby, by then."

"How about talking with the waitress at Billy's Bar and Grill, and the woman at the gym?"

"Do you know their names?"

"No, but I do know what they look like."

"Okay, let's go to Billy's and have dinner Saturday night. Maybe, she'll be there."

Task Force Bronner met Friday morning to discuss the latest information from Jesse. All the team members didn't think Maria was the killer, either. So far, Jesse was doing a good job staying close to Viper. When the task force decided to use Jesse, they gave him a code word to say if he was in trouble or to signal the police to move in, quickly.

The task force got some more reports from Heather. The DNA under Mrs. Bronner's fingernails matched Dillon Carr's profile, and the profile of the fetus proved Mrs. Bronner was carrying her husband's child.

Adam picked up Mabel at the airport around 3:00 pm. During the drive back to Nokesville, Mabel talked nonstop about her family and the Wisconsin winter. She told Adam her boobs stayed frozen the whole time she was up there. Of course, Mabel had to tell her daughter about the doctor telling her she was fifteen pounds overweight. Olivia told her mother she was proud of how hard she worked to lose nine pounds. She assured her mother the next six pounds would be a snap.

When Mabel told Olivia about Walt and line dancing,

Olivia fell off her chair laughing like a hyena. Naturally, Olivia teased her mother the whole visit about Walt, the bracelet man. Mabel told Adam if she didn't know better she'd swear Olivia was Millie's daughter.

Then, Adam had to stir the bucket of poop and tell Mabel Olivia was just like her mother. That was a big mistake, because Mabel just about cold cocked him with her power purse right there on the freeway.

Adam was glad he made it home alive, because Mabel was in a real snit when it came to Walt. He decided not to bring up Walt's name again, or Mabel was going to have a very serious hissy fit and tear him limb from limb.

Thank heavens, when she got inside the farmhouse, Timbo rushed up and gave her a big kiss and hug. Adam thought, "There goes Mabel melting like butter. She sure is a fuss and feather woman with a heart of gold."

Mabel knew Timbo liked football and baseball, so she bought him a Green Bay Packers shirt and a cheese head. He put the shirt on and modeled the cheese head for everyone to see. Timbo decided to wear everything for the rest of the day, and Adam and Mandy had to admit Timbo looked adorable and funny wearing his new things.

Mabel and Timbo proceeded to sit at the kitchen table while the boy told Aunt Mabel all about his new tutor and school schedule.

CHAPTER 14

Friday night, Hansa Fareed let Viper and Jesse in her apartment. They asked her about the con game, but she had no idea what they were talking about. She told them after a few dates she knew Dillon was a liar. If Dillon had any money, she believed he stole it from somewhere. She didn't believe the cabin in the mountains was his, either. As for his accidental death, she said he deserved it.

Once they left Hansa's apartment, Viper and Jesse talked about the visit.

Jesse said, "I don't think Hansa killed him, nor does she have the money."

Viper replied, *"When we asked her about the con game, she didn't have a clue what we were talking about. I agree; she's not our killer."*

Millie and Mabel were decked out in their cocktail dresses to go to Shiloh and Darren's wedding. The church service was at 4:00 pm, and the reception was right afterwards at the same hall that Dolly and Art used when they got married. The two ladies were looking forward to a delicious buffet and dancing the evening away with all those Freestone men.

Mabel thought, "At least, I don't have to put up with that twit brain, Walt."

Millie thought, "Too bad Gil wasn't invited, because he didn't know the couple."

The two southern belles didn't know it, but Shiloh invited Gil, Walt, and Mitch, so they could escort the ladies at the reception hall. Shiloh was a devious, southern belle herself, and she knew about the men being sweet on Scarlet O'Hara (Millie) and Ms. Magnolia (Mabel). Both Darren and Shiloh were anxious to see how much fur was going to fly at their reception among that bunch. This was going to be a knockdown, drag out wrestling match of emotions between that crowd, and Shiloh had a ring side seat to watch the Walt and Mabel circus.

The three men were in position at the reception hall door ready to ambush the ladies as they sashayed through the door. Gil jumped up and offered his arm to Millie who turned ten shades of red like a silly school girl. Walt and Mitch grabbed ahold of Mabel's arms and guided her over to the reception line. Mabel complained, "What the crap are you two doing here, because you don't know the bride and groom?"

Walt replied, "We were invited just like you."

"When Shiloh gets back from her honeymoon, I'm going to break bad on her."

Mitch shot back, "Play nice, Mabel, because you're surrounded. How many women do you see with two handsome, desirable men escorting them?"

"The number is none."

Walt chimed in, "All of us are going to eat a great dinner together and dance until we drop."

Mitch piped in, "All you have to do is be a good little girl and tough it out like a true southern belle."

"I won't make a scene, because I don't want to embarrass Shiloh."

Walt added, "There you go, Mabel, take one for the team."

"I'll dance with you, but only because I don't want you two to be male wall flowers."

Walt commented, "While we eat dinner, chew on the fact that Mitch and I want pictures taken with you two ladies in your lovely dresses."

"Stop blowing bull up my wazoo. I'll make sure I stick out my tongue when they snap the picture."

Mitch looked at Walt and said, "Walt, I think Mabel's brain froze solid when she was in Wisconsin or it's turned into cheese."

Walt replied, "I think you're right, Chief."

"What did I do to get dumped on by Mr. Twit Brain and Chief Crazy Pants?"

Walt remarked, "Easy girl, you don't want to run your blood pressure up and have a hissy fit in front of all these people."

"Up your wazoo, Weasel!"

The five of them sat down at their own table, feasted from the buffet layout, and enjoyed a piece of wedding cake. When the music started, Walt grabbed Mabel and escorted her onto the dance floor.

He held her tight and said, "Be a real good girl, because everyone is watching us. You don't want to kill me right here on the dance floor."

Mabel gritted her teeth and said with a big smile on her face, "You are driving me crazy, twit brain! I wish I could kick you all the way to Florida without breaking my leg."

Walt whispered in her ear, "No you don't. You look beautiful tonight, but you haven't said anything about how I look."

With a big, shit eating smile on her face, she said, "You look like a manure pie."

"Thank you, because I wanted to look my best just for you."

"You are so full of bullshit it's coming out of your ears."

"And you, my lady, have fire coming out of your nose."

"My blood pressure is shooting through the roof, because you are infuriating."

"Not so, Mabel, lust is shooting through your body and your cheeks are red."

"Will you shut up, so I can listen to the music?"

Lightly, Walt kissed her neck and whispered, "You can't fight my charm."

"If I wasn't a southern lady, I'd take my knee and rearrange your family jewels right here on the dance floor."

"No can do, Mabel, I wore a cup."

"Will you shut up and stop kissing my neck?"

"I would much rather kiss your lips."

"You're making my head spin, so I want some time out here."

"Okay, we'll hold each other tight and move with the music. Just don't pass out on me while I charm you."

Poor Mabel stayed frustrated the entire night, because she couldn't get away from Walt, Mitch, Vince, Art, and Dan. She knew it had to be a conspiracy cooked up between those jackass men.

When the music stopped, Mitch cut in on Dan for the next song. Mabel looked at Mitch and said, "Listen Chief, I'm a woman on the edge about two minutes away from having a nervous breakdown."

"No, you're not. You're fighting what your heart is telling you."

"Well, thank you very much for your crystal ball reading."

"Remember, I have the sight, and I see a wonderful woman who was married to three very good husbands who were taken away. You're afraid to love again, because you think this next man will leave you, too. Mabel, you give so much love to the people around you, savor every minute you have with them, and don't push love away. My Native American heritage has taught me to let your soul embrace love wherever you find it. Love is the goodness in this world, so don't ever push love away."

Mabel replied, "My heart was shattered when I lost my husbands. I don't think I have enough heart left to love."

"Do you love little Timmy?"

"Of course, I do!"

"Then, you just answered your questions."

The music ended, and Mitch walked away leaving Mabel standing there in a fog of emotion oblivious to the people around her.

Vince walked over to her and asked, "Is there something wrong, Mabel?"

"Vince, walk outside with me, please."

When the two of them stepped out in the chilly night air, Mabel took several deep breaths and said, "When my husbands passed away, I was devastated, and I swore I would never love another man, again. Vince, I'm sixty-one years old. I don't think I can love another man and put myself through that endless sorrow that descends around you when you lose the person you loved."

"Mabel, when Archie died, Bert was sent to you, so Olivia could have a wonderful father. When Bert died, Ray came to help you finish raising Olivia. Don't you see each one was sent to you for a reason?"

Right then, Walt rushed outside to see what was wrong with Mabel. Vince walked away as Walt rushed over and asked, "What's wrong, did I do something wrong?"

She looked at Walt and said, "I've tried everything I know of to run you away, but you won't leave. I don't know if I want another man after my marriages ended, so horribly. I'm damaged goods, Walt. My heart has taken a beating, and it still grieves. The last thing I want to do is hurt you, because I can't give you what you want."

Walt looked into Mabel's eyes filled with tears and said, "When my wife died, I did what Art pulled. I shut myself off from the world and almost ate myself to death, and I thank God everyday Art pulled me out of that dark hole of despair. Whatever, you can give me I'll take, gladly. Just don't push me away, please. You have a heart of gold, you make me laugh, and you have touched my soul. I know you care for me, because I can see it in your eyes."

"You can't see anything in my eyes, jackass!"

Gently, Walt kissed her lips for the very first time, and he knew she cared for him, because she kissed him back while he hugged her, tenderly.

He asked, "So, how is your nervous breakdown coming along, Pumpkin?"

"Can't you tell I've lost my pea picking mind, because I let you kiss and hug me?"

"I promise I won't tell a soul."

"We might as well go back inside and enjoy the rest of the evening, after I go to the bathroom before I pop."

"You read my mind, Ms. Magnolia."

Before the couple walked back inside, Art, Dolly, Vince, and Kris rushed away from the windows, so Mabel and Walt wouldn't know they were being watched. Shame on them!

Art said, "Did you see that? Mabel actually let Walt hug and kiss her right smack dab on the lips."

Vince replied, "Wonders never cease, folks."

Kris added, "She's trying so hard to run him off, but she just lost the battle."

Dolly chimed in, "Honey, she didn't lose the battle; she lost five wars, at least."

Art looked at Dolly and said, "Mabel reminds me of someone else I know."

Dolly fired back, "Oh shut your trap, Cricket!"

All four had a great laugh and then went back to the dance floor.

Viper and Jesse went to dinner at Billy's Bar and Grill, Saturday night. Jesse saw a waitress he knew, so he struck up a conversation with her.

"Hi girl, how are you doing?"

"I'm doing just fine, Jesse. Where's your usual buddy?"

"Well, something happened to him, and I thought I could find the waitress Dillon was dating to give her a message."

"You mean, Taylor?"

"Yep, but I don't see her."

"She's off today, but she'll be working Monday on the evening shift. She's really excited about the vacation she's going on for two weeks."

Jesse asked, "That's great! Where's she going?"

"That lucky skunk is going somewhere in the Caribbean to enjoy the beach, sun, and lots of booze."

Jesse commented, "I hope she has a wonderful time with her girlfriends."

"She's going to meet a man down there real secret like. Isn't that a blast? I tell you that girl is a trip. Well, let me take your orders, because I don't want you to leave here hungry."

As Viper and Jesse ate dinner, it was all Viper could do to keep calm and enjoy the food.

"That has to be her, and won't she be surprised when Dillon doesn't show up?"

"She could have killed him."

"That's right! That witch probably killed him, so she could have all the money. We have to get back here Monday and have a serious talk with her."

"Do you think she already has half the money?"

"At this point, I think she does."

"Why didn't she pull all the money out and double cross Dillon at his own game?"

"I don't know, but we sure as hades are going to find out."

"Are we still going to talk to Mrs. Newby?"

"Shit no, we have the right witch."

"Okay, Taylor works the evening shift Monday, so let's meet here for dinner and have a chit chat with her. I'm not above using force to get answers from the witch."

Jesse and the task force got together to discuss Monday's plan.

Hansen looked at Jesse and said, "We're pulling you for your own safety and to put Viper in a real tailspin. You did one fine job for us."

Jesse remarked, "Viper is zoned in on the waitress."

Gage commented, "We have you set up in a motel for a

few days and don't answer your cell phone. Viper is going to panic when you're not home or answering your cell phone."

Jesse said, "That's good, because Viper will go to Billy's place even if I'm not around."

Sunday, Viper called Jesse several times, but he never answered. When Viper drove by his house, the newspaper was still on the porch, and his car wasn't there.

"What the hades is going on? Is he dead? I bet that lowlife hooked up with that waitress witch! Did he kill her and has the money, now? Darn, I shouldn't have trusted that prick even though I didn't have a choice."

Viper went to Billy's Bar and Grill Sunday night, but neither the waitress nor Jesse had been there that day. Viper's blood was starting to boil. If neither one showed up Monday night, it was time to disappear and get out of the country.

CHAPTER 15

Monday was an important day for Adam and Erika. Adam got all of his things moved into the stone farmhouse and turned in his apartment key over the weekend. Today, he was going to see his surgeon to get the cast off his arm. He knew it wouldn't ever be normal, but he'd be satisfied with whatever movement he could get.

Erika was ready to go home after receiving such wonderful care at Millie's place. Dan was taking her home and promised his mother he would keep close tabs on Erika while she continued to recover. She was returning home to a clean, damaged repaired home with a new security system thanks to Freestone. Dan was going to help her set up her studio, so she could get back to work as a forensic sculptor. The FBI already had work for her when she was ready to start.

On the way back to Erika's home, Dan stopped at a grocery store, so they could fill up her refrigerator, freezer, and cabinets with food.

Dan commented, "I have a few days off, so I plan to stay with you, if that's alright with you. I promise not to attack you."

Erika laughed and said, "You can sleep in the spare bedroom or on the sofa. If you attack me, I'll just break a vase over your head."

Dan laughed and replied, "I think that's a good deal

between us."

When Dan opened her front door and she went in, she was stunned.

She said, "Everything looks wonderful and so clean. All the blood is gone. I can't see any damage, and the patio doors are gorgeous. I'll never be able to repay Freestone for all of their kindness and help."

"We don't need to be repaid. We want you to be safe and able to get your studio ready for business. I'm here to help you get a fantastic studio put together."

She replied, "I do have to admit I sure could use the help."

Dan and Erika got the groceries put away, and Dan insisted she lay down on the sofa and rest while he fixed dinner. They enjoyed dinner together, and Erika was pleased to see Dan was eating healthy. Millie told her to make sure he was eating smart.

She commented, "The meal was great, and your mother would be proud of you."

"Yes, Mom pounded that in my head, and I know she is right. I want to eat healthy, because I don't want bypass surgery in my future."

"You certainly are on the right track."

"We have to get your studio set up and get your home decorated for Christmas. Do you have any decorations?"

"I only have some lights and a few ornaments."

"That will not do, Ms. Erika! We have to get a tree, candles, wreaths, more lights, and more ornaments. We'll get your place all fixed up inside and outside."

"I do love Christmas, but since my husband died I've been hollow inside."

"I'm going to change your feelings, so you can enjoy Christmas, again."

They cleaned up the kitchen, watched a DVD, and decided to call it a night, so they would be ready to tackle the studio.

Dan put his things in the spare bedroom and took a shower while Erika got ready for bed. When he came out of the bedroom, she was in the kitchen taking some medicine. She was so pretty and elegant. He walked into the kitchen and got a glass of ice water.

He asked, "Do you have everything you need?"

"Yes."

"I want to kiss you goodnight, so if you object say so."

"I don't object."

Dan took her in his arms for the first time, planted a lights out kiss on her, and she returned the kiss with gusto."

He knew then that she cared for him, too. When they parted he said, "That was a mighty fine kiss. We should do this more often. If I wake up during the night, "I'll check to see if you're alright. Promise me you won't shoot me."

"I promise."

"Don't worry about breakfast, because I'll take care of that."

"I can cook breakfast."

"I'm going to pamper you for a while, so sit back and enjoy it."

"You are trying to charm me, Mr. Kramer."

"Darn, how did you figure that out?"

"I've been charmed before, Dan Kramer."

"How do I rate on the charm meter?"

"Somewhere between average and good, I'd say."

"It looks like I have to work harder. Oh well, I'm off to bed, so I'll be ready to tackle your studio."

They both said goodnight and headed to their bedrooms. Dan was true to his word, because he did check on her during the night, and thank heavens, she didn't shoot him.

The following day, Dan cooked another healthy breakfast they could eat together. Once the kitchen was cleaned up, the couple headed for Erika's studio to set everything up. When she looked around at the boxes she said, "I didn't have all these supplies stored in this room."

"Art decided to stock your studio full of the things you will need."

"I don't know what to say other than from the bottom of

my heart; he is a special man."

I think you can say thank you by giving him a big hug and kiss Christmas day at Mom's place," said Dan.

"It was so wonderful that your mother invited me, because I want to see Timbo go crazy opening his gifts. Plus, I want to see what happens between Walt and Mabel."

"Oh Lord, I don't want to miss that showdown for anything. The sparks will be flying between those two. I just hope they don't burn down my Mom's house in the process," Dan said laughing.

The couple had a big laugh and started opening boxes. They took a break to have lunch, and then went back to work. By the end of the day, they were pleased at how much they had accomplished.

The next day the couple went back to tackle the job and went to bed knowing they would be finished tomorrow.

Once the studio was ready for business, Dan and Erika went shopping for a Christmas tree and decorations. Erika couldn't believe how much Dan bought to turn her home into a Christmas palace. She really got into the Christmas spirit when they decorated her tree. She hugged and kissed Dan with gusto when the tree was finished. It was so beautiful it took her breath away. Then, to top it all off, Dan ordered several Christmas flower arrangements from the local florist. When they put them around the house, they were the final touch her home needed to scream Merry Christmas! She wouldn't have done any decorating if it wasn't for Dan. She realized Dan was filling up that hollow hole in her soul and heart.

The days they spent together convinced her that her future would be special and full of laughter. Also, she knew Dan would be in that future with her.

The 3M ladies were busy getting Millie's farmhouse, and the stone farmhouse ready for Adam and Mandy's wedding. Timbo was settled in a nice routine with his tutor and couldn't wait for the wedding and Christmas.

At the task force meeting, Heather brought them a report that seemed kind of strange. She found dog hairs on Dillon Carr's clothing when Warren County sent his remains to Freestone. She told the group the hairs belonged to a boxer, but Carr didn't own a dog.

When Hansen called Warren County, the Sheriff told him the investigator just finished talking to Carr's neighbor, and the neighbor owned a boxer Dillon played and rough housed with.

The day Carr was killed the dog kept running back and forth between their cabins like he always did. The neighbor and his family left to go home around 4:00 pm that day.

The Sheriff told Hansen there were animal footprints around the dry well, and when he compared the prints to the neighbor's dog they matched, perfectly. When the neighbor found out Carr fell into the well, he was shocked. The man did admit the dog had a habit of jumping on or knocking up against people. Warren County assured the man it was an accident, and they had no intentions of pressing charges or taking the dog.

When Hansen got off the phone, he told the group what happened.

Gage commented, "Then, it was an accident. Blow me over with a feather."

Ryan started laughing and said, "Viper is running around trying to find Carr's killer like a chicken with its' head cut off, but there's no killer. This is one crazy turn of events."

Just then, Jason walked in the task force conference room and dropped a bombshell.

"Hold on to your britches, because you're not going to believe this. John D. Meadows and his granddaughter Taylor W. Meadows are legitimate owners of a villa and land in Aruba. The grandparents retired and moved to Aruba fifteen years ago. Grandmother Meadows died three years ago, and John D. died two weeks ago. There is no way I can prove the money doesn't belong to them or Taylor. I don't know what Carr was trying to do, but he sure made a mess of things."

Hansen told Jason, "Put that money back into the account and take Taylor's name off the watch list."

"I've already done that, Boss."

Brad remarked, "That idiot thought he was going to impersonate granddaddy, take a bimbo to play Taylor, and empty the bank account. Boy, how stupid was that?"

Ryan commented, "This has been one screwed up case from the very beginning."

Byron added, "Now, we have Viper running around trying to find a killer that doesn't exist, money that wasn't stolen, phony passports, and a real Taylor W. Meadows."

Hansen spoke up and said, "Alright boys, let's go arrest Viper at work before our real Taylor W. Meadows is put in danger."

Gage added, "I can't believe how stupid Viper is. The idiot is making so many dumb decisions. I guess when some people smell money it turns them into stupid shits."

Hansen added, "We don't charge in like the cavalry; we walk into Bronner Pharmaceuticals and arrest Viper, quietly."

Karen Newby walked into Bronner Pharmaceuticals and headed for an office with a big smile on her face. She went into the office and closed the door behind her.

"Hi, Mrs. Newby, how are you doing?"

"I'm doing better every day. I got word you wanted to talk to me."

"As a matter of fact I do. Did you date Dillon Carr for a while?"

"I went out with him a few times until I found out he was a loser and a con artist."

"Did he ever ask you to go to Aruba with him, because he had lots of money in a secret account?"

"No, but he got really drunk one night and told me he killed my husband, because you hired him to do it."

Karen Newby took a pistol out of her purse and pointed it at Viper.

"Now, hold on here Mrs. Newby, because I didn't do any such thing. Carr was a liar and a loser."

"It's not going to work, because I know you did it. If you want to live, you better start answering some questions."

"I'm telling you I had nothing to do with your husband's death!"

Slowly, Mrs. Newby got up, walked behind the desk, and placed the gun barrel against Viper's temple.

"If you don't start talking, I'm going to pull the trigger, and your worthless brains are going to be plastered all over these walls. Now, why did you want my husband killed?"

"Dillon wanted to kill your husband, so he could romance you out of the life insurance money."

"Wrong again, because I was the only person who knew about that policy."

"Dillon told me he knew that policy was for a million dollars."

"Now, how could he know about that?"

Mrs. Newby cocked the hammer and said, "Say goodbye."

"Wait! Your husband manhandled me in the lab one day running his filthy hands all over me before I could get away from him. I told him I'd get even with him, and he just laughed at me and called me an uptight tramp."

"That's better. So, you were going to get even with him by hiring Dillon to kill him?"

"That's right, because he was an oversexed animal."

"Why did you send Dillon after Emma Baker?"

"I ran across those two screwing like rabbits in a storage room in the lab by accident. He looked at me, laughed, and wanted to know if I wanted to join them."

"So, you decided Emma had to be killed, too?"

"Yes, because she and your husband were sex crazy."

"Why didn't you go to the police about this when it first

started?"

"They would have laughed at me."

"I doubt they would have ignored your case. Why didn't you go to Dr. Bronner about this?"

"He made it perfectly clear when he opened the business that he wouldn't get involved in employee problems."

"Why didn't you say something to me?"

"You wouldn't have believed me. I can't understand why you stayed married to that cheating prick."

"We had a marriage of convenience. He did his thing and I did my thing."

"He was a prick that needed to be stopped."

The secretary alerted Detective Hansen that Mrs. Newby was in the office, so he had the secretary buzz the office. When the phone rang, Newby answered with the gun still resting against Viper's temple.

Hansen identified himself and told her why the police were there and said, "Please Mrs. Newby, don't do anything stupid. We have enough evidence to put her in jail for the rest of her life."

"Detective Hansen, I want you to walk into the office with

your hands on your head and close the door with your foot, very slowly."

Hansen did what Newby asked him to do, and he repeated, "Please, don't let this woman ruin your life."

"I have another question for this piece of trash. Why did you send Dillon to kill the Bronner family?"

"That was a mistake! Dillon screwed that up, not me!"

Newby said, "That family's blood is on your filthy hands, and I hope you rot in hades."

"That stupid prick screwed up my text message. He thought E B meant Emily Bronner, when I meant Emma Baker."

Hansen said, "Please put the gun down, Mrs. Newby. You don't want her blood on your hands. You have your whole life ahead of you. She's not worth it."

"You are responsible for a child's murder! Where is Timothy Bronner?"

"Dillon said he threw him down a dry well where nobody could find him."

"That means you have two children's blood on your hands."

"Detective, don't let her kill me!"

"Well, listen to you begging for your worthless life."

"Detective, you have to do something to stop her."

"Those people you killed didn't have time to beg for their lives. You are beyond pathetic!"

"Mrs. Newby, put the gun down. Don't let her turn you into a murderer."

"It's too late for that, because I want to kill her."

"Don't do this, because you will regret killing her."

Karen Newby pulled the trigger, and Dr. Clara Beach hit the floor. "She's all yours, detective, and you can have my gun, because it's not loaded. It's a shame the witch passed out, because I wanted to see the expression on her face when I pulled the trigger. I just needed some answers before I go on with my life. She was so smart, but she was one stupid killer."

Detective Hansen put the gun in his pocket before anyone else came through the door. Dr. Clara Beach was arrested and taken away. Hansen called Dolly with the great news, because little Timbo had his life back, now. When Dolly told Vince, Chad, and the Freestone agents who worked on the task force what went on, they couldn't help laughing from comic relief.

Dolly called Millie with the good news and told her to release the security detail. Millie walked into the family room and called for everybody's attention.

Millie looked at Timbo and said, "You don't have to be afraid anymore, because the police caught the bad person who took your family away."

Mandy launched herself into Adam's arms and cried tears of pure joy. Timbo ran over to Adam and Mandy as they both picked him up in their arms and hugged each other silly. Even Millie, Mabel, and Sheridan were mopping tears in their eyes.

Adam shouted, "I want to run around outside and scream like crazy." Next thing you knew, the three were running around outside, shouting, laughing, and chasing Pixie and Dixie.

December 19th was a crisp, cool day with lots of sunshine. Millie's farmhouse was decorated for Christmas inside and out like a Christmas wonderland. In the family room stood a large Christmas tree with enough decorations on it to sink a battleship. Finally, Adam and Mandy's wedding day had arrived.

Millie, Mabel, Mandy, and several friends had cooked and worked hard to create a wedding buffet fit for kings. Mabel's special project was baking the wedding cake and decorating it in secret. She just seemed to have a special talent when it came to wedding cakes.

Adam and Mandy spent the days before the wedding moving into the stone farmhouse. Several pieces of furniture came from Timbo's home, and the rest the couple bought. Timbo's bedroom and school room were all set up, so it would be a surprise for him. The couple even had the blinds, curtains, and pictures put up to give their new home an extra special touch.

They put their Christmas tree up in the family room, but didn't decorate it. They wanted Timbo to enjoy doing that with them. Mandy was sure he would recognize a lot of the decorations from his home, but the couple bought several new ones to put on the tree, too. Adam and Mandy wanted this Christmas to be extra special to Timbo, because he had lost so much in his short life. Mandy understood what he was going through, because she lost her mother, father, and brother who turned into a monster, serial killer.

Adam decided not to decorate outside until the day after the wedding. That way he and Timbo could work on the outside together. The couple planned to go on a honeymoon later, because getting Timbo settled and happy was far more important.

Millie, Mabel, and Sheridan got things ready for the wedding ceremony and the buffet. The flowers were set out leaving only the food left to put out after the ceremony.

The ladies put on their beautiful Christmas dresses while Adam and Cody helped Timbo get dressed in his tuxedo. Cody was Adam's best man, and Timbo was the ring bearer. When the men came downstairs all dressed up, the ladies had to admit they were mighty handsome. Of course, the ladies looked mighty fine themselves.

Vince and Kris were bringing Mandy with them. Kris helped Mandy get dressed in her wedding gown, and Vince had to admit Mandy sure was a pretty woman. Kris was

Mandy's matron of honor, and Kris was still drop dead, gorgeous as far as Vince was concerned.

The guests started arriving at Millie's farmhouse. Art and Dolly were stunning, and Art had the honor of giving Mandy away. Dan and Erika arrived right before the minister. When Nathan and Sierra arrived, she helped Millie arrange the gifts. Nathan, Dan, and Art slipped outside to decorate Adam's car for the big event.

Everyone took their places when Vince announced the bride had arrived. Art looked at Mandy and said, "You look beautiful! Are you ready to begin a new life?"

She said, "Yes, but I'm so nervous."

He laughed and said, "Dolly was nervous, too. Don't worry honey, you'll be just fine."

Mandy walked towards the family room on Art's arm. When Adam saw her, he was stunned. She looked like an angel in her beautiful gown. He had to keep telling himself not to go weak in the knees or pass out. Timbo looked at her and thought she was an angel, too.

The ceremony was wonderful, because the minister's words touched everyone's hearts. Even some of the men brushed back tears. Timbo saw his mother next to Mandy and heard her whisper in his ear, "She will be a wonderful mother to you, and Adam will love you like your father loved you. Be a good son, and Greta will watch over you." When the couple kissed, the guests clapped their hands and laughed with joy.

After dozens of pictures were taken, the ladies set out the buffet and told everybody to dig in. When Mandy saw her wedding cake for the first time, tears ran down her cheeks. She had no idea Mabel could create such a masterpiece. She hugged Mabel and told her how wonderful it was. Of course, Timbo had to sample the icing with his finger when no one was looking.

After the guests feasted at the buffet, Adam and Mandy cut the gorgeous cake. Adam couldn't believe how much cake Timbo ate. With everything else he ate, he must be ready to pop.

Today, Mabel decided she was going to eat as much as she wanted. There was no such thing as a diet on a wedding day.

Once the group finished pigging out on the cake, the couple started opening their wedding presents. All of them were wonderful and needed. The best gift of all was the official adoption papers Art handed to them. Timbo was now their son! When Timbo understood what those papers meant, he jumped up and down, ran around hugging everybody, and launched himself into Mandy and Adam's arms. Lots of folks wiped tears, because they couldn't understand why they were so sentimental.

Nathan caught the garter, and Erika caught the bouquet. As the couple headed for Adam's car, the guests threw bird seed at them. Vince picked Timbo up and said, "Adam and Mandy are going over to your new home to set up a surprise for you. They need some time to get it ready. All of us want to hear you play the piano, and we want to line dance, too. You need to teach Kris and me how to line dance like you did for Millie and Mabel."

"Sure, I can do that."

Everybody changed into comfortable clothes, so they could all dance. Now, Erika and Sheridan could dance some after recovering from their injuries.

Three and a half hours later everyone ate a snack, and Mabel fixed up a goody box for Adam, Mandy, and Timbo for their dinner. The group pitched in to clean up everything and put stuff away. All of them ended up with goody boxes to take home, too.

Everybody visited for a while longer, and then the guests started leaving for home. Vince and Kris stayed a while longer before taking Timbo to his new home.

Vince carried the box of goodies up to the door and knocked. Shortly, Adam opened the door and the three walked in. Timbo stopped dead in his tracks when he saw the Christmas tree. Adam took the box of goodies while Vince and Kris slipped out the door. Mandy stepped out from behind the tree and shouted, "Surprise!"

Timbo ran up to the tree and asked, "Is this our very own Christmas tree?"

"You bet it is!"

He asked, "Where are the decorations?"

"They're in all of these boxes. We are going to decorate it together."

He hugged Mandy and started opening the boxes. He

realized a lot of the ornaments came from his home.

Mandy added, "I hope you don't mind us keeping your family's Christmas ornaments."

"Thank you a lot. Some of these balls came from Germany and are very special." He hugged Mandy and kissed her cheek.

Adam spoke up, "Let's start decorating this tree, Timbo." The boy laughed and all three started putting the ornaments on.

Later, Mandy said it was time to take a break and eat some dinner. They laughed and ate, so they could get back to the tree and finish it up. When they were done, they stepped back to admire their handiwork.

Timbo said, "It's the best Christmas tree ever. It's better than Aunt Millie's tree."

Adam answered, "I agree, Timbo. Tomorrow, you and I are going to decorate outside, so your mom can wrap presents."

Timbo shouted, "I can't wait until tomorrow!"

Mandy said, "Now, it's time for you to find your bedroom down that hallway."

Timbo ran down the hall and went into every room until he found his. Several minutes later he ran back to the family room and said, "My bedroom is almost like it was before, the Harry Potter poster is great, and I got my own bathroom! I got a school room, too. I love everything and my new home."

"We love it, too, Timbo."

The next day after the wedding, Cody got Sheridan all packed up to move back into her apartment that she shared with her sister, Sierra.

Sheridan would be forever grateful and indebted to Freestone, Millie, and Mabel for taking such good care of her when she was injured. She knew in her heart Freestone saved her life when they found her in that ravine. Also, she knew she was falling in love with Cody, because he was a wonderful man with a kind heart. She prayed he would care as much for her as she did him.

Tears flowed between Millie, Mabel, and Sheridan as she thanked them for all they had done for her. As far as she was concerned, these two ladies were angels. She promised to stay in touch and come back to visit often. She was even going to miss the wild kingdom, Pixie, Dixie, and Mr. and Mrs. Greedy Gut. They hugged, kissed, and wiped tears as Cody and Sheridan headed for his truck. She wanted to bawl like a baby, but she struggled to keep her composure. Everyone waved as Cody drove away from the house.

Cody took her hand and said, "Don't be sad, because we'll visit often. You know, those two ladies feel like my grandmas, and I bet you feel the same way."

Sheridan just couldn't help it; she nodded yes and bawled like a baby. Cody laughed and put his arm around her. Finally, she got control of her emotions and said, "I'm glad to be going home. I've missed Sierra a lot."

"I'm sure she has missed you, too."

When Cody and Sheridan walked into her apartment, Nathan and Sierra shouted, "Surprise!"

Lord, their apartment looked like a Christmas show place. Sheridan couldn't believe how beautiful the Christmas tree was. She knew Nathan and Sierra must have spent a long time decorating it. She hugged both of them and told them how much she loved them. She told them how wonderful the apartment looked all decorated. They both smiled, because Nathan and Sierra wanted to really surprise her.

Nathan and Cody brought all of Sheridan's things in, and Sierra helped her put them away. Since Sheridan hadn't done any Christmas shopping, the foursome decided to go shopping, and eat dinner out to celebrate Sheridan's return. The bunch shopped until Sheridan said she was hungry.

When the group sat down in the restaurant, Sheridan told them about the promise she made to herself when she saw that deer running away from serial killer, Lonnie Baldwin. They all laughed and Cody told her to order the biggest steak on the menu and eat all she wanted. Needless to say, Sheridan ordered the porterhouse steak with a baked potato and salad. She didn't have enough room to put away the whole steak, so she put the rest in a doggie bag to go.

At dinner, Nathan informed everyone that they were all invited to spend Christmas Day at his parent's house. They all agreed to come, because Nathan wouldn't take no for an answer.

After the guys kissed the girls goodnight and left, the

sisters hugged each other and plopped on the sofa.

Sheridan remarked, "Sis, Freestone has changed our lives forever. We have met lots of incredible people that have welcomed us into their arms and lives."

"I know. Freestone is like a family, because everyone cares about one another."

"We have a new family just like Timbo."

"Sheridan, I don't know about you, but I want to enjoy every minute of this new happiness."

"Amen to that, Sis."

Cody didn't have to go back to work until after Christmas, so each day he spent with Sheridan getting ready for Christmas. He hadn't had this much fun in his entire life. He knew deep down in his soul that Sheridan was his destiny. He didn't want to rush things, but he knew he was going to marry her one day. She told him she was going to change her major in college, because she wanted to be a forensic sculptor like Erika. He admired her decision and told her to follow her dream.

Art and Dolly spent Christmas Eve with his family. They all gathered at Ken's house to enjoy a holiday dinner and open their Christmas presents from each other. Dolly told Ken's wife how wonderful their home looked all decorated.

The Christmas ham plus all the trimmings were delicious, and Dolly really enjoyed the pumpkin pie. She thought the pie was the best she had ever eaten with Mabel's pie a close second. All the grandchildren ate until Dolly was sure they would explode. The grandchildren cleared the table and helped Teresa and Ken's wife clean up and put everything away. Dolly wanted to help, but the granddaughters told her no, because she was a very special guest and their new grandmother.

When everyone gathered around the Christmas tree in the living room, Ken did the honors by passing out the present. Once all the gifts were passed out, he told everybody to dive in. Dolly looked around at all the children as they ripped open their gifts and shouted from excitement. This was something she never experienced, because she was an only child, and Desiree was her only cousin. Even her first husband was an only child, too. She enjoyed listening to the chatter and laughter.

The special Christmas ornaments she and Art bought for each family member caused a fury of hugs and kisses. Art and Dolly were given a list from everyone to make shopping for them a lot easier. They got everything on the lists, but the ornaments surprised all of them. Art glanced at Dolly amid flying bows and paper and smiled. He knew this was a first for Dolly, and he wanted her to drink it all in and enjoy.

Ken and his sister, Teresa, were taking lots of pictures, because there was something different this Christmas. Their father was happier than on any other Christmas they could remember. Their children buzzed around Dolly like bees to honey. Sadly, Ken and Teresa had to admit their own mother just wasn't like Dolly one bit. Their mother was quiet, reserved, and had trouble expressing her feelings. Dolly was loving, funny, and loved to laugh. The children just loved her, because she hugged, teased, and talked to them. She didn't care if the little ones wanted to crawl up in her lap. There was something very special about this woman, and they were so glad their father found her and fell in love.

When it was time to leave, Art and Dolly said their goodbyes with hugs and kisses. On the way back home, Dolly told her husband what a wonderful time she had. He was so glad his family had welcomed her with open arms and genuine love.

The following day Dolly and Art spent their first Christmas together as man and wife. Art was treated to his first extra-special Christmas with the woman he truly loved. Dolly and Art gathered around the Christmas tree with Rosarita and Ernesto and opened their gifts like little children. Shouts and laughter filled the room with the spirit of Christmas.

The four treated themselves to a lavish brunch before Ernesto and Rosarita left to celebrate the holiday with his brother's family. Dolly and Art would eat Christmas dinner with Millie, Mabel, and all the other guests. Both were looking forward to the feast the ladies always put on. There would be a house full of family and friends, but they were anxious to see how Walt and Mabel were going to act. They didn't know if Mabel was going to slap him dizzy or just prance around him. Oh yes, they wanted a front row seat to this soap opera.

Mr. and Mrs. Donovan invited Sierra, Sheridan, and Cody to spend Christmas with them. Nathan's parents really liked the two sisters, and they knew Sierra was good for their son, because she understood what he was going through to adjust to being at home, again. They enjoyed Christmas dinner and ate until everyone was ready to pop. They exchanged gifts and acted like little kids around the tree.

Both girls were given special gifts from the men in their lives. Cody gave Sheridan a beautiful diamond heart necklace which blew her away. Nathan gave Sierra a gold opal bracelet that took her breath away. The girls enjoyed this wonderful holiday with people they knew cared about them. This holiday their father didn't ruin things for the girls like so many times in the past. The sisters were able to embrace a very special time in their lives.

Early Christmas morning, Millie and Mabel shared a special breakfast just for the two of them. They opened their Christmas presents to each other like two kids and laughed until they were silly.

This Christmas there were several new people to add to their guest list. Both ladies were anxious to see how Timbo was going to deal with Christmas without his parents and sister.

Millie said, "I think Timbo will be alright, because he loves Adam and Mandy. He'll feel safe and special with them."

Mabel added, "I bet that little tike is running around like crazy opening his presents. By the time they get here around lunch time, he'll be bouncing off the walls."

Millie remarked, "You know, Mabel, I had no idea Adam would take to the boy like that."

"I didn't either, but I'm glad Adam had his life changed by our Mandy and little Timbo."

Millie added, "Just see what happened to Vince when he married Kris."

"Praise the Lord, honey child!"

The sisters giggled like school girls as they cleaned up the breakfast dishes and got things ready for lunch.

Pixie and Dixie were fed, but they weren't looking forward to this day, because Millie made them wear Christmas bows on their heads. Sometimes, people could do some of the dumbest things. They just hated wearing those dumbass bows. The only reason they put up with it was to get some really good, chewy bones to eat. Both of them couldn't understand why they couldn't get under the tree. They liked watching the lights blink, too. So what, if several ornaments fell off the tree and got broken. They couldn't help it if their tails knocked a bunch off the tree. Well at least, this crap only happened once a year.

Millie and Mabel got dressed up in their fancy Christmas outfits. This was a holiday tradition going why back when they were in high school. Millie always wore a red dress accented with silver, and Mabel always wore a green outfit accented in gold. Of course, Mabel's holiday earrings were big and wild.

It wasn't long before Timmy ran through the front door shouting, "Merry Christmas!" He was wearing his new Christmas outfit, and he modeled it for the ladies. He hugged and kissed the ladies, then said, "Oh, I forgot I got to help Dad bring in the presents. I'll be right back!" He tore out the front door like a tornado and grabbed some packages. The threesome came inside carrying lots of gifts. Adam and Timbo went back outside to bring in food for the banquet.

Mandy looked at the ladies and said, "I wish you could have seen him last night and early this morning. Last night he asked us if he could put all of his presents together, so he wouldn't miss any, today."

Millie asked, "When did he get up this morning?"

"Would you believe at 6:00 am? He doesn't get up that early for school. He ran up and down the hallway shouting, Merry Christmas, until Adam and I got out of bed and staggered into the family room. Poor Adam wandered into the kitchen and put a pot of coffee on, because he knew we needed that pick up."

Mabel asked, "Does Timbo ever walk anywhere?"

"He doesn't walk much, and I don't understand where he gets all the energy to run all over the place. Once Adam and I got a cup of coffee, we let him tear through the presents. Wrapping paper and bows were flying everywhere, and he was shouting, Merry Christmas, every time he opened a present. Adam and I haven't had that many hugs and kisses in our entire lives. He even went nuts over his Pirates of the Caribbean poster and T-shirt."

Mabel added, "Don't forget, Jason and Sierra run all over Freestone when they get excited."

"That's right! Mabel, you shouldn't have let him buy those presents for us. Christmas is for the children."

Mabel put her hands on her hips and scolded, "You listen to me, Mandy Cobb, he wanted to give you those gifts; I thought it was a great idea, so both of you need to suck it up."

"I surrender! After we ate breakfast and got dressed, he took his new sheet music over to the piano and played until we came over here."

Millie remarked, "Well, he's going to go crazy opening his presents here."

Mabel called out, "Timbo, it's time to feed Mr. and Mrs. Greedy Gut their holiday meal."

Timbo grabbed the plate and rushed to the patio doors to await their arrival. Adam put their gifts around the tree and joined Timbo.

Mandy commented, "I can't believe you didn't put a bow on top of a peanut butter jar for the happy couple."

Mabel fired back, "Up your wazoo, Miss Smarty Pants!"

The ladies put lunch together while those two in the family room laughed like monkeys swinging through the trees.

Millie blessed the food and told Mabel she better not think about a diet today, or she would beat her over the head with a turkey leg.

Around two o'clock their guests started arriving. Dan and Erika hugged and kissed everyone, and Dan put their gifts around the tree. He took his mother aside and showed her the beautiful emerald necklace he gave Erika for Christmas. Millie noticed Erika glowed while wearing it, so she knew good things were in the future for her son and his wonderful lady.

The routine was repeated when Dolly, Art, Gil, and Byron arrived to be greeted with the sights and smells of this holiday season.

Timbo wrapped himself around Dolly and Art and shouted, "Merry Christmas, Nana, and Pop-Pop."

Of course, for the next few minutes Art tickled him dizzy.

Gil looked at Millie and said, "You look mighty pretty in your holiday dress. You're a Christmas present all by yourself."

Millie turned ten shades of red and thanked him for his compliment. She didn't realize she was standing under the mistletoe until Gil and Byron kissed her. She slapped Byron's arm and said, "Get on with your bad self!"

Byron laughed and gave her a big bear hug.

All the friends and family were waiting for Walt and Mitch to arrive. About ten minutes later, the two arrived to be greeted by lots of hugs and kisses.

Timbo wrapped himself around Mitch's legs and shouted, "Merry Christmas, Chief Crazy Pants!"

Mitch roared with laughter, picked him up, and tickled the boy silly. "May you have a Merry Christmas, too, Chief Line Dancer."

Everyone roared with laughter while Timbo jumped up and down with joy. "I love my new nickname; I'm Chief Line Dancer." Of course, he performed some of his fancy moves for everybody.

Mabel looked at Walt and thought he was quite handsome in his blue slacks and red sweater. "Why am I thinking this shit?"

Walt walked over to Mabel and said, "Merry Christmas, Mabel. You look stunning in your holiday dress, and I'm going to steal a kiss whether you like it or not."

He kissed her cheek while everyone held their breaths waiting for Mabel to kick Walt into the crackling fireplace. What's this; she let him kiss her? Well, it was just a little kiss on the cheek. She had to play nice and be a southern lady.

Now, Millie and Mabel had a tradition about Christmas presents. The family and friends that came for Christmas dinner drew names. No one was allowed to buy everybody a gift. However, this year they made a concession, so everybody could give a gift to Timbo. What the sisters didn't know wouldn't hurt them. Some wheeling and dealing went on behind their backs. Gil bribed Dolly to get Millie's name, and Walt bribed Erika to get Mabel's name. What was wrong with bribing one's friends, because the men wanted their ladies' names?

The group gathered around the tree, and Byron was elected to pass out the gifts. Again, paper and bows were flying everywhere, and Timbo was on a serious cookie high. Every time that boy opened a gift, he ran around showing everyone what he was given. When Timbo opened up Mitch's gift, the crowd roared with laughter at the T-shirt that read, "Chief Line Dancer."

When Millie opened her gift from Gil, she was shocked. He gave her a gazebo bird feeder with a gorgeous watch inside. She could tell the watch was not cheap. She walked over to him and kissed his forehead as she blushed or was it a hot flash?

All eyes shifted to Mabel as she opened her gift from Walt. She opened up the box and inside was a magnificent pair of diamond teardrop earrings she knew was expensive. She turned several shades of red, gave him a kiss on the cheek, and thanked him for the wonderful gift. What's this? She didn't throw him into the tree and beat the crap out of him. The others knew Mabel was up to something, because she could be a devious smart butt when she wanted to be.

The Christmas buffet was served and everybody filled their plates full from all the goodies. Timbo must have eaten a pound of mashed potatoes along with turkey, green beans, a slice of red velvet cake, and two brownies. Art and Dolly thought the boy was going to explode any minute. When everyone was finished, they were ready to pop, too.

They took a break from the feast and gathered in the family room to sing carols while Timbo played the piano. Quick as a flash, Mabel pulled Walt into the pantry, because they had some serious shit to talk about.

Mabel looked him in the eyes and said, "You cheated, because I know you didn't draw my name!"

"I had your name in my hand, Smarty Pants!"

"I can't accept the present you gave me. You spent way too much money on them."

"Do you think the earrings are ugly?"

"No, they're gorgeous."

"Mabel, those earrings are worth every penny I spent to have your friendship."

"You are driving me crazy, you pest!"

"Well, stop fighting my charm!"

"You are no Prince Charming, Weasel!"

"And you are no Cinderella, Pumpkin!"

Mabel planted a quick kiss on his lips and stomped out of the pantry. Walt laughed, because he knew he won this boxing match. Plus, he didn't even get a black eye from it.

When the day came to an end, the guests carried goodies from the buffet with them, as they said their goodbyes. As he walked to his car, Walt stole another quick kiss when Mabel wasn't looking. Everyone hugged and waved goodbye, got into their cars, and Millie and Mabel's family and close friends drove away.

All of them wondered what happened between Walt and Mabel when they disappeared for a few minutes. What were those two sly foxes doing? Obviously, Mabel didn't beat up Walt or dump him in the fireplace. Alright, they would have to wait for the next showdown to happen.

Mabel wasn't pushing Walt away as she tried to adjust her life to this new relationship. She just didn't know if her heart would let her love, again.

Mabel and Walt's relationship will be tested when they go undercover for Freestone to smoke out a stalker that is trying to kill world famous architect, Wesley Mansfield, and the woman he loves.

Coming Soon

WHO IS STALKING ME?

World famous architect and widower, Wesley Mansfield, Jr. is getting tired of one high society woman after another trying to drag him to the altar. Then, one evening he sees a pretty woman reading and giving teddy bears to the children in a hospital wing he designed.

Suddenly, his life changes when bizarre events start happening to him, and the woman he's falling in love with. It's, then, that Wes realizes he is being stalked.

At a Wounded Warriors picnic, Wes asks Freestone for their protection. Freestone must figure out how many people are stalking him and why, so he can have the woman he truly loves. Mabel Langley, one of Freestone's 3M ladies, goes undercover to smoke out a stalker. Look out high society women who want to be snobs, because Mabel is ready to do battle and put on an Academy Award winning performance southern style from the genteel class.

ABOUT THE AUTHOR

Faye Benjamin was born and raised in Virginia where she still lives with her husband and black cat "Spooky." She enjoys creating her stories and wants to share that joy with those people who love to read. So, readers sit back, relax, laugh, and enter her Freestone's world of murder, mystery, intrigue, humor, and the paranormal.

Made in the USA
Charleston, SC
25 April 2014